THIERRY'S ANGEL

SHARA AZOD

Cacoethes Books are published by

Cacoethes Publishing House, LLC.
14715 Pacific Avenue South
Suite 604
Tacoma, WA 98444

Contact our office for units for bulk purchases for sales promotion, premiums, fund-raising, educational or institutional use.

Special book excerpts or customized printings can also be created to fit specific needs. For details, write or phone the office of the Cacoethes Sales Manager: Cacoethes Publishing House, LLC., 14715 Pacific Avenue South, Suite 604, Tacoma, WA 98444. Attn. Sales Department. Phone: 253-536-3747

ISBN: 978-0-9816190-0-2

Printed in the United States of America

Can the power of his love and the magic of his touch make her believe in happily ever after again?

THIERRY'S ANGEL
©2007 Shara Azod

In New Orleans, where old Southern lineages root as deep and tangled as the haughty Cypress, two powerful families become entrenched in a battle to preserve pedigrees. For the past nine years, Thierry Chevalier, the strikingly handsome, well-bred, polished son of one of the oldest, most powerful white families in Louisiana, has been harboring an impassioned desire to captivate the woman of his dreams. His desire, Angelique Dubois. Graceful, delicate and sensually delectable, Angelique seems as unattainable as she is desirable: the daughter of New Orleans' mayor; member of a proud Black Creole family; and engaged to another man. But when opportunity opens, their fates are magnetized. The tempest of passion, power and pride that erupts is more sweeping than a steamy Gulf Coast monsoon.

Cacoethes Publishing House, LLC.
14715 Pacific Avenue South
Suite 604
Tacoma, WA 98444

Thierry's Angel
Copyright © 2007 by Shara Azod
Cover by PK1 Studios
Photography By Michelle Anderson
ISBN: 978-0-9799015-0-8
Ebook ISBN: 978-0-9799015-1-5
www.cacoëthespublishing.com

First Cacoethes Publishing House, LLC. Electronic publication: November 2007

DEDICATION

This book is dedicated with love to Auntie Alma, who opened my eyes to the wonderful world of romance and believed in me before anyone else, and my loving husband Mark for all his support and for never letting me give up on my dream.

I would like to thank Ana Maria, Dahlia and Marianne for all the no-nonsense advice, my editor Dyann Gregg for working with me, and my best friends Dirty Red and Darkness for listening to my crap.

The meeting of two personalities is like the contact of two chemical substances: if there is any reaction, both are transformed.

~Carl Jung

<u>Acknowledgements</u>

Thank you to the great state of Louisiana for your

continuous inspiration.

CHAPTER ONE

Angelique covertly watched the couple at the adjacent table with envy and more than a little yearning. Both seemed to be roughly her age, maybe a little younger. They were sitting side by side as close as they could get, though no one else occupied their small café table. The man could not seem to keep his hands away from the woman. He touched her hair, her cheek, her legs, and her arms. Their kisses had started off innocently, almost like a question, but had grown in fervor. Angelique wondered how either of them could breathe. The woman was flushed, squirming in her seat while the man looked nowhere else but at his ladylove. What must that feel like to be desired in such a way? To have someone so into you they blocked out the entire world, as if you were the only thing in the universe that meant anything at all to them?

"Angelique, are you listening? I swear your mind is always in the clouds somewhere. And I don't understand why you would want to live on your own in that old house. You'll only have to move again after the ceremony. I am quite sure Paul would never want to live in that neighborhood!"

Paul, her so-called fiancé, had never looked at her the way the unknown man looked at his woman. He had never touched her in a way that made her burn.

"It doesn't seem be at all safe—especially now, after the horrible hurricane," Charline Dubois continued, completely unaware her audience was anything but captive. "I don't understand why your father would agree to let you buy that house. I can't imagine what you might have said to him to make him agree with such a foolish decision. What if something were to happen to you? Where would you be then? Just think about all the things you'll have to do to make that place habitable . . . I mean, it is a complete waste of money!"

Angelique stirred her coffee absently as her mother droned on and on. There was little point in interrupting or adding anything to the one-sided conversation. She would just ignore her anyway.

"And look at your hair! It looks positively nappy. I don't understand how you could come out so . . . Well, you look nothing like *me* or *my* family. I don't understand where that hair came from. And just look at your skin! Have you been using the fading cream I gave you? You are going to have to remember to stay out of the sun! You look positively bronze!"

Some people would love to look positively bronze, Angelique thought to her herself. Of course, she said nothing out loud. Meeting her mother for shopping and coffee had been a huge mistake. When Charline Dubois had called claiming she missed "her little girl," Angelique felt that twinge of hope she had fostered all her life: maybe this time Mother would be different. Maybe they could just hang out and at least be civil to one another. Not that

Angelique was ever anything but obedient and compliant as

far as her parents knew. It still was not enough for her

mother, who felt the need to point out everything wrong or

undesirable about her at every opportunity. Her hair was

too nappy, she was too dark, too naïve, too bookish.

Angelique was not the perfect Creole daughter Charline

had wanted. Instead of the dusky ivory-and-cream skin and

"good hair," Angelique had skin that was an interesting

mixture of browns and reds, like milk chocolate swirled

with cinnamon and a touch of Kashmir saffron. Rather than

having light-colored eyes to declare her mixed linage, her

eyes were dreamy brown. Soulful eyes, her grandmother

called them. Plain mud brown was all Charline saw.

      The Dubois clan was a proud Black Creole family.

Her father, Adam, was currently the mayor of New

Orleans. His father had been the first African-American

mayor. The family owned a multitude of businesses and

properties throughout the state. They could trace their roots back through Creole *gens de couleur libres* to one Amélie Durand, who was the daughter of an African slave and some kind of French nobleman. Family legend had it that she married the illegitimate son of a French king. Angelique doubted most of the story was true, but it was pleasant family folklore. Her mother, however, believed every word. She reveled in it, flaunted it whenever the opportunity presented itself. The woman lived and breathed Dubois pride—which Angelique found a bit odd, seeing as her mother was only a Dubois through marriage. It seemed that the family name meant far more to Charline and Anne, her aunt by marriage, than it did anyone else.

"Angelique Marie, are you listening to me?"

God, how she wanted to say, *No, you aren't saying anything worth listening to.* Instead, an apology sprung to her lips without thought.

"I'm sorry, Mama. What were you saying?"

"I said you should go down to the office and see if Paul would like to have lunch with you today. It would be a pleasant surprise, and you two have rarely been seen out in public since the engagement announcement. You really should more effort into this relationship; I don't see how you even got him to propose with the way you act. I will make a hair appointment for next week with Irene. She always seems to be able to tame that wild mane you call hair. You want to look your best for your engagement ball."

Angelique wanted to scream she hadn't gotten Paul to propose, she'd never wanted him to. It was the implied promise of political and business advancement Charline placed into his head on numerous occasions that made the man ask her out and finally to marry him. She wasn't entirely sure she even liked Paul Guidry. Sure, he was fine, with his light golden skin, devilish dimples, bright hazel eyes, and tall, well-muscled physique. Yes, he said all the right things, dressed nicely, and had a great education. But when all was said and done, he was her mother's choice. He came from a suitable Creole family, he belonged to all the right social clubs, he had a small fortune of his own, and he and his mother were intimidated by the Dubois name. Paul was everything Charline had ever dreamed for in a son-in-law. He had even proposed at the dinner with her parents present, as if he knew she would probably have said no had they been alone—which they rarely were.

"That's a great idea, Mother!" Angelique exclaimed brightly. "I think I'll go right now so I can catch him before he gets roped into a boring business meeting."

She didn't give her mother a chance to reply, just grabbed her bags and purse and practically ran out of the little café. What made her think she could stand her mother longer than ten minutes, she'd never know! Maybe one day she'd learn and stop expecting anything more from the vain, selfish woman. Charline had wanted to shop with her today to be seen and ensure that Angelique was dressing appropriately, and to remind her of the upcoming engagement ball. How many times had she heard today, "Honestly, Angelique, you are either dressed as a vagabond or some kind of whore." She was wearing jeans and a designer shirt. True, neither was remarkable, but she felt comfortable. They had spent almost an hour going over the guest list. Well, Charline had gone over it. Angelique had silently assented to whatever her mother suggested.

She waited until she was around the corner to hail a cab. Her mother would flip if she saw her getting into what she referred to as "dirty contraptions," but she would be damned if she would call for a car from her parents' house, nor would she take her own car; that would only serve to waste gas and frustrate her as she looked for parking. She got out on Lasalle Street to walk to Perdido, where her father kept his business offices near city hall. Paul had worked for him at city hall, but had resigned after their so-called engagement a month ago. He was now a business director for Dubois Enterprises.

To avoid fake well-wishes or intrusive questions, she slipped into the building from the back, waving at the maintenance crew as she took the service elevators up to the top floor. By going this way, she could avoid the receptionist and all the other managerial and executive offices. The service elevator opened in the back corner of the building. Angelique noticed Paul's secretary wasn't at her desk, so she decided to walk right in. He might be in a meeting, but even if he were, he would be pleased by her initiative to walk in as if she owned the place. Well, she did own twenty-five percent of all Dubois Enterprises' businesses and properties, but Paul would want everyone who was anyone to know she was his fiancée. He loved to flaunt the fact that he was engaged to the boss's daughter. It didn't matter to him if the other executives hated him or thought he had only gotten his position through nepotism.

What mattered was that he had power none but the old man could dispute.

Had Angelique stopped to listen at the door, she might have knocked; but her mind was on other things. It took a full minute for her to realize what was going on right in front of her face. Paul had Tasha, his secretary, bent over his desk as he plowed into her like there was no tomorrow. With both of their backs turned, neither noticed her standing there dumbfounded as they rutted like a couple of dogs in heat.

"Oh, God, yessss! Give it to me! Fuck me harder!" Tasha was panting as Paul burrowed into her over-inflated ass.

"You like that, don't you?" he demanded. "You like all of this big, fat dick!"

She should have been offended, Angelique realized with a start. She should have been furious to see her fiancé going at it with the secretary *she* had convinced him to hire.

Paul had wanted at least a college graduate: "someone with a little class," he had told her. One of the many charities Angelique was involved with helped find jobs and homes for people displaced by Hurricane Katrina. Tasha didn't have much experience in the workforce, no family, and no prospects. She could type well and had taken diction classes in high school, so Angelique had decided to get her a job here. No one else was going to take a chance on the woman if she didn't gain some experience. Angelique had begged until Paul relented, agreeing to hire her on a trial basis. That had been a little over six months ago.

I guess they're getting along well enough, Angelique thought, slipping out of the office before she was noticed. She would be lying to herself if she said it didn't hurt to see the man who supposedly loved her so much he wanted to make her his wife fucking his secretary, of all people. What a fucking cliché. But the tears that began to silently fall from her eyes were not because Paul was cheating on her. She had known he was sleeping

around almost from the beginning. All of the signs had

been present: the phone calls he abruptly ended whenever

she was around, the lipstick on the collar. It wasn't the fact

that he couldn't keep it in his pants that disturbed her.

What really got to her was the fact that Paul had

never given her more than a peck on the cheek. No matter

what she did, he had never seemed sexually interested in

her. Whenever they went out, Paul usually preferred to

have people around. At first it hadn't bothered her; she

knew what this relationship was about, and love or even

physical attraction had nothing to do with it. But after the

proposal, she had tried on numerous occasions to get some

kind of sexual reaction from him. She tried rubbing her

body against his, but he always moved away, pretending

nothing had happened. Then she tried not being fully

dressed whenever he came to pick her up for a date, but he

didn't seem to notice. In fact, whenever they went

somewhere with her friends, his eyes were often on them and rarely on her.

Angelique didn't have much experience in the romance department, but she did know that her love life had always been lacking. Not even as a teenager had any of the young men she dated even attempted to step over the line. The few rare times she had actually taken the initiative and become the aggressor, every one of the men she had dated had backed off, seemingly embarrassed by her wantonness. She used to think it was because of who her father was, but lately she had begun to wonder. Maybe she was just not sexually attractive. After talking it over with and taking the advice of Regina, one of her best friends and a clinical psychologist, Angelique had confronted Paul.

"Do you find me attractive?" she asked him one night as he was driving her home from a charity function.

"Of course I do." His answer was automatic, but he didn't even glance her way.

"Then why is it you have never even tried to kiss me?"

Paul looked uncomfortable, squirming in his seat as his eyes darted from the traffic ahead to his hands, the steering wheel, then back out into traffic. Everywhere but at her.

"I've kissed you," he offered lamely.

"Sure, on the cheek, but never a real kiss. How can you want to marry someone you don't even know you're compatible with?"

"Of course we're compatible," Paul sighed, clearly annoyed with the conversation.

Angelique was not about to let it go. "Sexually? I mean, do you even find me attractive?"

Surprised, he swung his head around to look at her. His eyes traveled over her face, down to the cleavage pressing against the provocatively-cut evening gown, over her torso to her legs, then back at traffic.

"Uh, yeah," he managed to choke out. "You are attractive. I mean, I find you, uh . . ."

"Doable?" she supplied hopefully.

Paul cursed softly, but did not confirm. "Look, Angelique, you know you are a beautiful woman. It's just that I know you're a virgin, and I want to wait. There's nothing wrong with a woman saving herself for marriage, even if it is rare. I just want to wait for that night, okay? Let me show you that much respect."

And that had been the end of that. Angelique still didn't know just how Paul had known she was a virgin, and she hadn't asked. The subject had never come up again. But it was the awful feeling that she was somehow lacking that made her make a fateful decision that night.

The following day when she met her friends for lunch, she told them what she intended to do.

"You are crazy!" her cousin Solange had informed her. "If anyone in the family finds out . . . Angie, it would ruin your father!"

"No one is going to find out, Sollie!" she insisted. "And if they do, I will assume you opened your big mouth."

"Why would you want to do this, Angel?" Jade, a lawyer and New York native who had come to New Orleans for college and never left, asked. "I don't understand."

"I understand," Katrina, Jade's law partner, spoke up for the first time. "You can use my place outside of Lafitte. It's my only members-only gentlemen's club; most of the patrons there are white, filthy rich and have a lot to lose. No one should recognize you properly masked, and if they did, they would never say a word. It's part of the contract they sign to be admitted."

"But stripping, Angie? Are you crazy?" Solange insisted, ignoring Katrina altogether, as she often did. For reasons Angelique could not begin to understand, Solange had never liked Katrina. Probably because Katrina, unlike the Dubois clan, could not trace her roots back any further than her mother, a drug-addicted tramp who lost custody of Katrina when she was six years old. Katrina was from Nevada: a former foster kid with a government grant to attend St. Xavier, as the entire group had for undergrad. Angelique had tried to talk to Solange about it, but the Creole woman could be excessively hardheaded at times.

The women had all become fast friends as college freshmen, and had stayed friends through graduate school; Katrina and Jade at Tulane, Angelique and Regina at LSU, and Solange at Loyola. Now Jade and Katrina were high-priced, high-powered corporate lawyers—though Katrina also owned some strip and fetish clubs throughout Louisiana—Regina was a psychologist, Solange owned a chic French Quarter boutique, and Angelique…well, she was a debutante. She volunteered, was on the board of numerous charities, assisted her mother in hosting events, and dreamed of life beyond family obligations. To tell the truth, Angelique was suffocating.

"I understand too," Regina had said. "Paul has placed some serious doubt as to her sexuality, her sense of personal allure, if you will. I mean, it's not like she'll be sleeping with a bunch of unknown men. It's only dancing. It could be healthy for her."

Solange snorted, rolled her eyes, and proceeded to become engrossed in everything but the conversation at hand. Angelique and Solange were as close as sisters, but sometimes Solange could be exceedingly self-absorbed.

"Really," Regina continued, "I think it might be a good thing for your self-esteem. It might make you feel like the attractive woman you are."

"Shit, girl, you're hot!" Katrina insisted. "I think maybe some men are just a little intimidated, you know? Anyway, we'll be there with you whenever you decide to dance. If stripping will make you feel better, I'm just glad I own the club where you can do it safely. Trust me, if Paul can't see how sexy you are to every guy that looks your way, he's gay."

Angelique had been doubtful when Katrina first said that, and she was even more so now she had seen Paul fucking his secretary, who was very much female. Gay men didn't fuck their female secretaries.

She thought about calling the girls for emotional support, then immediately decided against it. She was a grown woman, damn it! She could deal with this herself. Besides, she really didn't want to share with anyone how pathetic she felt. Only one thing could make her feel better, and this time she would do it alone.

Hailing another cab, she made her way to her own home, the one her mother hated, in the area that was once used for rich white Creole men to house their mistresses of color. Angelique loved the Faubourg Marigny neighborhood. That was the real reason she bought the house here. It made her feel some weird connection with the women who were reputed to be all things sexual and enticing. It gave her a thrill. Sighing in pleasure as she entered her house and began planning her night, she imagined the ghosts of the past watching her, encouraging her to grab onto her sexuality, to revel in it. She guessed that's why she found so much pleasure in dancing. And, to her friend's surprise, she was good at it. Very good. She made a small fortune in tips every time she was on stage. She always gave it to charity anonymously, but it felt good to be desired.

Much later, she slipped into a cab to take her as far as Lafitte. There she would take another cab to Kat's

Meow, the most exclusive gentlemen's club in Louisiana.

Tonight, she would dance.

CHAPTER TWO

Thierry hadn't wanted to go out with his cousins tonight, especially not to some strip club in Lafitte, no matter how exclusive. It wasn't like there weren't strip clubs in New Orleans. They could even have gone into Baton Rogue if Remy, whose brilliant idea this outing was, hadn't wanted to stay in town. His cousin had sworn this place, the Kat's Meow of all ridiculous names, was the place to be for the men of wealth and power all over Louisiana and beyond. Of course Thierry had already known that. He was a member, after all. Not that he would ever admit to any of his cousins. The place was much more than a strip club, but he was unsure if Remy knew that.

Thierry had grown somewhat degenerate in his pleasures of late. He tried any and everything to still the burning hunger inside of him. The insatiable need for something he could never have. At the club, it was easy to find watered-down copies of his true obsession, and it would do for now. God only knew how long that would last.

So he had agreed to go, seeing as how he had nothing better to do on a Friday night. That was, unless he wanted to let his veritable dragon of a grandmother drag him to some social function or another, where she would no doubt try to not-so-subtly push him towards some hopeful former debutante. At thirty-five, he was a little old for an actual deb.

Before Remy called, Thierry had planned on being comfortably ensconced with his mistress in his newly purchased and renovated play cottage on Pauger Street, in the famous Faubourg Marigny neighborhood in the heart of New Orleans. It was perhaps perverse to buy a place to explore every aspect of his growing sexual deviancy where octoroon and quadroon *placées* were kept by their patrons before the Louisiana Purchase. The English had seen these women as little more than "colored mistresses," but they were in essence more then lovers; they were second wives, best friends, and so much more to some men. These dynamic women were an intrinsic part of the history of the city and the state. They were, in reality, the foremothers of Louisiana.

He supposed that's why he just couldn't stomach actually bringing his now ex-mistress Marsha into the delightfully large cottage. True, he hadn't exactly planned on giving her walking papers just yet. She was a blonde, voluptuous garden of sensual delight, which he had truly enjoyed exploring. However, looking into those baby blues that sparkled with greed and schemes more than any lust he might have inspired, he knew there was no way in hell he could share his love nest with her. Its cheerful yellow exterior with light-blue trim, lush and colorful courtyard garden with a small kidney-shaped pool, elegant mahogany-accented interior complete with a harem-inspired bedroom, gourmet kitchen, and even a formal receiving parlor demanded a real lady. Somehow he hadn't created the sexual playhouse he had intended. This was a home, one in which he would share more than just a sexual relationship. Thierry realized—with a healthy dose of despair—that he'd striven to make every aspect of his remodeled cottage just right for one woman. The woman he had watched and ached for from afar for the better part of seven years now. The one woman in the world he could never, ever have.

Shit, he was beginning to sound like a fucking *Lifetime* movie. What kind of man restored and redecorated a house for a woman he had never actually met in person? For that matter, what kind of man kept a scrapbook with every news clipping and every photo printed of that woman for nine years? He was turning into some kind of stalker freak. This obsession was going to have to end soon, or he might do something colossally stupid. He simply had to find some way to work this woman out of his system.

Not for the first time in his life, Thierry cursed the fates that had decreed he be born a Chevalier, one of the oldest, most powerful families in Louisiana. His grandfather had been both a governor and a United States Senator. His father, Beaumont Chevalier, was now one of the Senators representing the great state of Louisiana, and had been one of the first old Southern Democrats to formally switch to the Republican Party during the 1960s. His family was by far one of the richest in America, settling in the state directly from France and bringing with them a good amount of wealth and power. However, with all the wealth and power came responsibility: to the family name, to the party, to society in general.

At least, that was what his grandmother had drummed into all of their heads since birth. His mother had had very little to do with his upbringing. Arienne Chevalier, called Lady Rienne by one and all, had made it her personal mission to raise all five of her grandsons—

much to the dismay of their mothers. Those who complained too much or too loudly quickly found themselves ostracized. No one dared gainsay Lady Rienne. Especially not her three sons. Thierry and his cousin, Piers, were her favorites. Thierry could understand her affection for Piers. Piers was the political heir apparent, poised to win his first race for Congress, groomed to take the place of Thierry's father when he finally retired. Thierry, on the other hand, ran several of the family's businesses. He was admittedly something of a financial genius, able to see market shifts before they happened with uncanny accuracy. He had quadrupled the family fortune several times over, and he hated every minute of it. How much money did one family need? His children's children would never have to work a day, even if the market were to crash tomorrow. It was all so pointless, primarily because no amount of money or power could win him the one thing he craved. The woman who'd starred in his most erotic dreams since she turned sixteen. Angelique Marie Dubois.

Though they lived in the same city, he had never even spoken to her, but he knew damn near everything there was to know about her. He knew her favorite foods and restaurants, her best friends, who she dated. Ever since he had seen her when she was little more than a child, Angelique had always fascinated him. It wasn't until he watched her televised cotillion that his fascination turned into something more. Watching her in her virgin white, smiling sweetly as she was presented, had him masturbating for a week. He cursed himself for the sick bastard he knew himself to be, lusting after a sixteen-year-old. He was ten years her senior, for God's sake! Still he found himself dreaming of her milk-chocolate skin kissed with hints of red and gold; his hands itched to see if it were as silky and smooth as it seemed. He longed to have those deep brown eyes looking at him with love and adoration, or better yet looking up at him, filled with longing. Not that he had ever seen her look that way to anyone, not even her philandering fiancé. Thierry had made it his personal business to keep tabs on every aspect of her life, paying a fortune to out-of-state private investigators to learn everything there was to know about her. Too bad it was an exercise in futility.

Shaking off his maudlin thoughts, Thierry left the condo he kept in the Quarter to pick up Piers. Forever worrying about his image, his cousin had unequivocally stated that if he were going out for a night of debauchery, it wouldn't be in one of his highly recognizable cars. Thierry had to pick him up from Lady Rienne's home in Bayou St. John.

"No one can see me leave," Piers had insisted. "You have to drive into the garage so no one will see me get into the car. Anyone watching will think I spent the night with Grandmother."

Thierry shook his head. If becoming a part of the real family business, politics, meant worrying about someone watching your every move, Piers could have it. None of the gossip columnists would dare report on anything Thierry did. They were all terrified of invoking his wrath. At twenty-five, some poor reporter had gotten it into her head to follow him around, reporting his every liaison. Thierry had bought the paper and fired the woman without blinking an eye. When she had gone to another paper, he bought that one too and fired her again. She had then tried her hand at a local television station, only to find herself fired again when local sponsors abruptly pulled ads. The woman had finally moved to someplace far away. After that, most reports concentrated on Thierry's philanthropic endeavors or rare society appearances, staying far away from his personal life. Piers had to be far more careful. His cousins Aubrey and Rance never did anything worth reporting. Remy simply didn't give a damn.

"Aren't you going to go inside to say hello to Grandmother?" Piers asked when Thierry pulled into his grandmother's massive garage, motioning for his cousin to get in the car.

Glancing at the door, Thierry felt a compulsion to be away from this house as quickly as possible. Shaking his head, he put the car into reverse before Piers could settle into the passenger seat.

"Hey," Piers drawled, laughing at his cousin's haste. "I could ask why you're in a hurry, but I'm afraid I know."

"Yeah, why am I in a hurry, then?" Thierry wanted to know.

"She's matchmaking again. She has no less than five eligible women in there right now."

"I think that was more for the future congressman than for me."

Piers grimaced but said nothing. Not for the first

time, Thierry wondered whether Piers even wanted a career in politics.

"I haven't announced I'm running yet," Piers muttered, gazing out of the window.

"You're running, golden boy."

Piers remained silent, looking broodingly out of the window. He wasn't frowning exactly, but Thierry could tell something was bothering him. The problem was, Piers wasn't one to talk about what he was feeling. He was the only person Thierry had ever met—besides himself—who was in complete control all of the time.

"Piers." Thierry had to search for the right words to say. He wasn't very good with the whole heart-to-heart thing. "If this isn't something you want to do... Well, don't let the family drag you into something you don't want."

"You mean like you?" Piers asked softly without turning.

Touché. Thierry detested his job as the CEO of LeBlanc, Inc. The company had endured since 1765, inherited by a Chevalier wife who was the only child of Pierre LeBlanc, who was rumored to have made his money from piracy. It had expanded from the original import/export company to an international conglomerate with companies and interests ranging from to real estate to manufacturing and retail, not to mention an interest in pharmaceuticals and biotechnology. And running it all was Thierry. Buying, selling, breaking up or building new companies, negotiating new partnerships. To the world, he was a captain of industry. A cold, calculating businessman who could and would buy and sell with cold-blooded efficiency. To most of the Chevalier clan, he was the rock who ensured their financial supremacy and opulent lifestyle. To Piers, Remy, Aubrey, and Rance, he was a brother-in-arms against a world of mortal enemies. It had always been them against all others, even members of their

own family.

"Yeah, well, if you want to talk about it . . ."

Thierry left the rest unsaid as he pulled into the parking lot

of a decidedly understated building. "This looks more like a

warehouse than a strip club," he muttered as he

maneuvered his car to the far corner of the building. For

Piers' sake, he decided to forgo the valet parking he spied

in front of the building.

"You never heard of this place before?" Piers asked

incredulously. "I hear it's the place to be. Everyone who is

anyone belongs."

"Do you?" Thierry snapped. He hadn't meant to be

short, but this was *his*

playground, damn it. It was something he didn't think he

could explain to anyone, not even the four people closest to

him.

"No, but I have heard about it."

Well, if Piers had heard of it, he supposed it was perhaps time to rethink his membership. Piers didn't know anyone outside the right social circle. Not anyone he would talk about a strip club with, anyway. Although Remy had suggested the place, Thierry doubted he had spent much time here. His membership was probably new, and given Remy's attention span, the place would soon bore his wild cousin.

"We're late; the others are probably already inside." Thierry said, changing the subject. "Let's get this over with."

Piers looked askance at his favorite cousin. "If you didn't want to come, why did you agree? *I* only agreed after Remy told me you were coming."

Thierry sighed and decided to tell the unvarnished truth. "I had nothing else to do."

Aubrey, Remy, and Rance were inside waiting for them at the bar on the ground floor that held a regular dance club.

"Is there a reason for this little gathering?" Thierry drawled after they had moved to a booth.

Remy smiled, lifting his glass. "Why, gentleman, we are here to celebrate Aubrey's sudden freedom!"

Piers gaped at his brother. "You're getting a divorce?"

Remy erupted into hysterical laughter at the incredulous faces around the table. Aubrey, a professor of history at Tulane, might be absent-minded, often forgetting the outside world when he was researching some long-dead culture or another, but he was nothing if not steady and faithful. His wife of ten years, Susan, seemed the understanding sort. She was a quiet little mouse, never interfering or bothering her husband when he was engrossed with a project.

"She left him," Remy cackled while Aubrey turned bright red.

"Shit, Remy, that's not funny," Rance, the resident lawyer and Remy's brother, scolded. "Has her attorney contacted you yet? She realizes with the prenup she gets nothing, right?"

Remy was now laughing so hard he almost fell out of the booth. "She left him three months ago," he managed to wheeze, holding up a letter. "The professor here probably would never have noticed if she hadn't sent him a letter. Get this, she's been at some mission in South America for two months, and Professor Brilliant here never knew she was gone!"

Piers, Aubrey's brother, snatched the letter, reading it while Rance and Thierry crowded around him to look. All three men looked up at Aubrey in awe as Remy tried unsuccessfully to smother his laughter.

"She's been gone for three months and you didn't notice?" Piers demanded.

"Aubrey, it never struck you as odd how quiet the house was?" Thierry asked incredulously.

"You never noticed you were alone in the bed at night?" Rance piled on.

Aubrey downed his bourbon in one gulp and shrugged. "I have kind of been sleeping in my study lately. I hadn't seen Susan recently, but . . ." He shrugged again, not bothering to finish. He felt guilty, but it wasn't because Susan had left. All in all, he was relieved that she was gone. He hadn't loved her, certainly not the way she deserved to be loved. That caused the shame and remorse more than anything else. Susan had been Lady Rienne's pick for him. Aubrey, far more interested in the past than anything in the present, had simply gone along with it rather than to be constantly badgered about his bachelorhood. Piers, Rance, Remy, and Thierry might have had the stomach to stand up to the old girl, but he never could.

They were silent while Thierry ordered another round of bourbons.

"Well you can't possibly miss her that much if you didn't even notice she was gone," Rance muttered as he downed his drink. "I'll file first thing Monday. Don't reply to the letter. I'll take care of it."

"I told you not to marry her," Piers offered. "The woman had no passion."

"Like you would know passion," Remy snorted. "You're so damned uptight, I bet you have your underwear pressed."

"Well, are we going to sit here all night, or are we going upstairs?" Thierry interjected, changing the subject. No sense in crying over spilt milk. They all agreed Aubrey was better off. Love was never much of an issue in their circle, but companionship and even friendship was nice.

Susan often seemed so remote; it was as if she were never really there. According to the letter she'd sent, she wasn't. She had bowed to the dictates of her family by marrying Aubrey. Now that her parents had passed away, she felt free to do what she had always wanted to do: work with the poor in far-off places.

"What the hell do you know about upstairs?" Remy asked Thierry suspiciously.

Oh, well, Thierry thought to himself. There was little use in keeping his secret now. Aubrey needed to let loose a little bit. Pulling out his V.I.P. card, he offered Remy a smirk. "Gentlemen, get out your checkbooks and follow me."

CHAPTER THREE

Angelique exhaled, trying to prepare herself for her next set. Maybe she shouldn't have come, not without Katrina at the very least. For some reason, she just wanted to do this alone tonight. She needed the reassurance and rush she could only find on the stage, and she didn't want to share that with anyone just now. Adjusting her teal and gold-feathered Mardi Gras mask, she critically inspected her similarly-colored outfit made up mostly of sheer scarves. Most of the regular girls who worked the third level garnered a private dressing room complete with a large couch to rest or entertain admirers. House rules were the door must be open if fans wanted to visit with a dancer backstage. Katrina insisted she was not running a whorehouse—not here, anyway.

Given that membership included the regional director of the FBI, several congressmen, and some well-connected businessmen, there was little chance of the Kat's

Meow ever being raided. Not to mention that Katrina cut

the local police in on the profits. Membership fees were

rumored to cost upwards of six digits, depending on the

type of membership.

There were four levels to the club. The first floor

was just an average club were the beautiful and the

nouveau riche mingled. Though that was members only, it

only cost a couple of hundred a month. The second floor

was the first of two strip clubs. While of higher caliber than

your average strip club, it was relatively tame by southern

Louisiana standards. The girls went no further than their g-

strings. You could look but not touch. It was for those who

aspired to be rich and powerful. The third and fourth floors

were what really brought in the money.

The third floor was where Angelique was now.

Here exotic dances were seriously exotic and could lead to

complete nudity or just what amounted to a bikini. The

women who worked here were true artists, most of them

professional dancers. The fourth floor was a private sex club where the women were not only beautiful, but free. It was really more like a sort of dating service for those looking to hook up with someone with similar kinks. Katrina had said they catered to everything from harmless public sex fetishes to hardcore BDSM. Membership fees were never discussed, but if you had to ask you couldn't afford it. Members were allowed to bring their own guest or try their luck at finding someone there, but anyone who entered had to sign nondisclosure agreements. Angelique had never been there. She was curious, but Katrina wouldn't let any of them up there.

"Hey, I rarely go up there myself," she had shrugged when all the girls had tried to get her to take them up. "Trust me, you aren't missing anything. Just a bunch of lonely people doing what they feel they need to do to make it through the night."

It was a crock, but they had let it go at that. Katrina was an enigma. She owned strip clubs, fetish clubs, and a couple of brothels, but she could be downright prudish about some things, especially within their group of friends.

"Why do you do it then?" Regina, forever the shrink, had asked.

Katrina shook her head. "Maybe I'm working out my demons, Doc."

She was fiercely protective, which was one of the reasons Angelique didn't want to call her. The manager hadn't been too happy to see her without Katrina, but he would get over it. He knew better than to say no.

Solange had been convinced that Katrina had been a prostitute in Nevada, but no one paid her much attention. Now Angelique wondered what Katrina got out of this besides money. It wasn't as though Katrina was hurting for cash.

Angelique knew why *she* was here. It wasn't so much about Paul and what she had seen today, but about herself. She wanted so much to be wanted; she needed to be wanted. No one had ever looked at her as anything more than an extension of something else, generally her father or her family. The men who asked her out had always had some kind of ulterior motive. She was so much more than the mayor's daughter or an aimless debutante. She was more than a Dubois. She wanted affirmation, and here the crowd roared for her and her alone. Men panted when she swayed; they threw ungodly amounts of money at the stage because she never deigned to stoop to get a bill shoved into her thong. The tension was always palpable whenever she finished a set. Who knew the twenty-five-year-old virgin daughter of the mayor was a natural at stripping?

***

Taking charge of the night's entertainment, Thierry led his cousins to a table right in front of the stage at the

51

end of the runway. After several bottles of Pappy Van

Winkle's Family Reserve 20-Year Bourbon, even Piers had

begun to relax and enjoy the show. Deciding that Aubrey

really needed to get laid and forget about his misplaced

wife, Thierry was about to suggest they move the party to

the fourth floor when the next performer danced on stage.

Her face was covered with a feathered mask reminiscent of

Brazilian Mardi Gras; her body was artfully draped in sheer

scarves, placed in such a way that the spectator was

titillated by glances of the skin beneath without revealing

the most intimate places. A sensual Middle-Eastern

inspired jazz melody filled the air as the dancer began to

move slowly, hypnotizing almost every eye in the room.

She swayed seductively with a natural rhythm as old as

time, an elemental enticement meant to torment and

beguile. As the first silken scarf floated to the ground,

Thierry felt his blood freeze in his veins. Although he

could only see the chocolate-cinnamon colored leg up to

her thigh, he instinctively knew that leg. One after another, the scarves glided to the floor of the stage, and he became more certain those were *his* legs, *his* thighs, *his* hips.

The anger built like a slow-moving tsunami, threatening every ounce of his renowned control. He didn't have to glance around the room to see the pants of every Tom, Dick, and Harry in the bedamned audience. She was Delilah in the flesh; Salomé sent to enthrall the unsuspecting. There was no need to see her face to know that the dancer was Angelique Dubois herself. What the fuck was she doing stripping here, of all places? Of course he knew that one of her friends owned the club, but surely her friend wouldn't be so reckless to let the beloved daughter of New Orleans strip?

"Damn, I think I need to invite her upstairs with us," Remy muttered as the last veil fell.

She wasn't nude, but then she didn't need to be. As she whirled to her finale, what was left of her outfit—tiny golden disks woven together to create a bra-like top and a barely-there skirt—clung to her like a second skin. He could hear his cousins muttering in approval. As she collapsed in an artful little heap on stage, Thierry carefully set his glass down and, without looking at his cousins, rose to his feet as she exited the stage.

"I am afraid the *lady* is unavailable tonight," he replied softly. He couldn't look at any of their faces; if he did he might have to hurt them.

"Aw, come on, Thierry," Remy persisted. "We all saw her at the same time. Besides, she's hardly your type. I say we invite her have a drink and let her decide which one of us she would like to spend the evening with."

"Or two," Rance muttered, quaffing another drink.

Many people considered Remy the debauched member of the Chevalier clan. However, every one of the five cousins had a healthy dose of sexual profligacy, and Rance was probably the most perverse of them all. Most people never looked beyond his station as one of the nation's top attorneys or his military background, but Rance was into things that would make Remy blush. There was no way in hell Thierry would ever let him within a hundred yards of Angelique.

Thierry had to take deep breath and let it out slowly. *They don't know, they couldn't know*, he reminded himself.

"You misunderstood," he replied, turning a face devoid of any emotion towards Rance and Remy. "She was unavailable before she stepped on that stage. Please excuse me, gentlemen. Something seems to have come up. Aubrey, I'll call you tomorrow; have a good time tonight."

All four men watched their normally staid cousin stroll off, flabbergasted.

There was a small office located at the back of each level with its own manager. The manager of this section was a shifty little weasel of a man. It didn't take much to have him escort Thierry back to the dressing rooms.

Though patrons were allowed to visit dressing rooms at the dancer's consent, he knew there were probably standing orders that this particular dancer was never to have visitors. It didn't do a thing to still the fury raging underneath his calm facade. What if it had been someone else who didn't want to take no for an answer? Many of those degenerate bastards in the audience had wanted her as soon as she began to dance. Hell, who wouldn't? When she danced she was pure temptation, a vertical reminder of the horizontal dance of creation. What if he hadn't been here tonight? The ass of a manager would have let just about anybody back here without a second thought. Thierry had to clench his jaw tightly to keep from growling. He made a quick mental note to deal with the man—later. His hands were clenching sporadically by the time the man he was seriously considering killing and dumping into the bayou knocked on her door. He had to bite the inside of his cheek when the asshole just opened the door and swept his hands as if he were inviting Thierry into his own damn home. He hadn't waited for her reply.

Angelique whirled, clutching her shirt to her bare bosom, as her dressing room door opened without her consent. The night manager, Tim, entered, followed by a patron. Thank God she'd at least had a chance to put on her jeans.

"I don't take visitors," she told him coldly. "Please leave."

"See here, missy, this nice gentleman just wanted to meet you," Tim sneered. "Why don't you be a good girl and talk to him for a spell. Customer service is important; otherwise I can't rightly say I need you to be working my shift."

Angelique understood the implicit threat. The bastard knew she hadn't danced tonight with Katrina's knowledge. If she wanted him to keep her secret, she would do as he said. There was no way of knowing whether or not he knew who she was. Chances were good that he did. If she had the courage of someone like Katrina, she would have told him off and thrown them both out of her dressing room. Even as the thought coursed through her head, she knew she wouldn't do it. She just wasn't the type for confrontations; it wasn't in her nature. Cursing herself for being a coward, she lifted her chin and faced Tim.

"I will *talk* to the gentleman," she hissed through clenched teeth, "when I am dressed—outside."

"Now see here . . ." Tim began, only to be stopped by a none-too-gentle hand descending on his thin shoulders.

"Why don't you leave now, Timmy?" Thierry suggested in a way that let the other man know it was no suggestion. "The lady and I will be just fine without your assistance."

He really wanted to kick the shit out of the little weasel, but he had to use him to get to talk to Angelique.

Thierry's hands clenched spastically into fists, itching to punch the night manager in the face just once. The bastard would probably have let anyone into her dressing room for the right price.

Angelique felt all the blood rush from her enflamed cheeks as she belatedly recognized her visitor. Shit! If Thierry Chevalier recognized her, this could be all over Louisiana before sunrise. Her father would be disgraced, his career likely ruined. Her mother would never let her live this down! Maybe he hadn't recognized her yet, she thought, frantically looking around for something, anything to hide her face. Shit! Shit! Shit! How could she have been so stupid? She should have never come here alone! Katrina would have been all too happy to come with her, if she had only asked. Now she was, quite literally, screwed. All too soon, Thierry had escorted Tim out of the dressing room and closed the door.

"Why are looking so panicked, Angelique?"

So much for not knowing who she was.

"What do you want?"

Thierry frowned at the defeated sound of her voice. She probably thought he would threaten her or gloat about finding her here. There was little doubt, judging by the forlorn look on her face, that she thought he would expose her. Her head hung, her shoulders slumped. Damn it, this was not what he wanted at all! He had to get her out of here so he could explain to her all he wanted was to talk a little, away from the social constraints that usually bound them, and away from all the horny men in the front room who would only want to bend her over.

Thierry raised his hands in mock surrender. "I'm not here to make trouble for you, Angel. I really think you need to get out of here, though. I recognized you easily; how do you know someone else won't?"

Angelique's body stiffened as her eyes narrowed.

"And why would you care?" she demanded. "What exactly do you want for *helping* me get out of here unnoticed?"

Well, hell. This was going from bad to worse. Now she thought he wanted to blackmail his way into her pants. He had every intention of getting into those pants, but not the way she seemed to think.

"I didn't mean it the way you think I did," he muttered, taking a step back. Looking down at the way she was still clutching her shirt to her bosom, he turned around. "Maybe you should put on your shirt, then we'll talk."

All was silent for a few seconds before he heard the sounds of her moving quickly into the shirt.

"You can turn around now."

Thierry turned and smiled.

"Maybe we should sit a spell," he gestured towards the couch.

Angelique shrugged and plopped down, eyeing him warily as he sat as close as he could without crowding her.

"Look, like I said, I don't want to make trouble for you," he began, thinking furiously of way to get her to relax. "When I saw you on the stage, I just had to save . . . That is, I just wanted to make sure no one else realized who you were and maybe take this opportunity to, uh, talk."

Now he was starting to sound like some wet-behind-the-ears schoolboy. Damn, what this woman did to him. She was more lethal in the flesh. His cock was so hard it hurt just being in the same room with her. His hands itched to reach out and touch her. He had to try to get some control before he did or said something even more idiotic.

"I'm not doing this very well." Thierry ran and hand through his hair as he tried to think of what to say. "I've wanted to get to know you better for a while, but we've never really had an opportunity to be friends. I was just excited you were here tonight so I could finally do it."

Smooth and urbane it was not, but it was the truth, and he decided to go with it.

Angelique watched the man next to her with a mixture of trepidation and fascination. He seemed sincere, but she had never heard much positive about the Chevalier clan. They were a ruthless lot. There was no love lost between her family and theirs, so what was this man's angle?

"Why would you want to be my friend?" Angelique asked, not quite certain she believed him, but not at all sure if he was full of it. "We hardly move in the same circles."

Thierry decided to go for broke. "Who wouldn't be your friend, Angel? I mean
. . . shit, I'm not doing this right." Blowing out a deep breath, he looked into her eyes and took her hands. "When I saw you, I couldn't think of anything other than getting you out of here and away from those assholes out there. I know it looks bad, me barging in here. I'm just glad it was

me and not some other…" *Some other guy just like me*, he thought wryly, but could not bring himself to say it.

He didn't want a quick lay with a stripper in the back of a club. He wanted *her*, in every conceivable way.

He moved closer until their legs were touching. Reaching out, he caressed her cheek. "Look, I know everything I say sounds a lot like some lame-ass line. Seriously, I wouldn't want to see you hurt in any way."

Angelique's breath caught as he leaned forward. He was going to kiss her! If she had any sense, she would move away. It was probably a set up, and Lord knew she didn't need to compound her disgrace. But Lord, he was fine! He was taller than he seemed in photos or on television, around six-three. His jet-black hair set of his unusual turquoise eyes to perfection. Those eyes were now looking at her with an intensity she had never experienced before. It sent chills racing down her spine. He seemed enthralled with her skin; he hadn't stopped touching her, but rather, moved from her cheek to her eyebrow, down to her ear, then her throat. The light caress made her tingle.

"What do you really want?" Angelique asked, swallowing hard.

Thierry blew out a harsh breath. What could he say that wouldn't make her run away screaming? It was weird that they'd never really met before; but then, they came from very different sides of elite society. He had met her father, of course, and her mother very briefly, but he had only seen Angelique on television or in an article. Their lives may have been parallel in a way, but they were miles apart.

"Look, I know we've never met and you have no reason to believe me, but I just want to make sure you get home safely," Thierry told her earnestly. He didn't say that he wanted to see her safely to *his* home. She was spooked enough as it was. "I swear, I just don't want anything to happen to you."

"Why?" She seemed genuinely surprised and confused as to why he would care.

"I think you're special." He shrugged. "A genuinely nice person. I wouldn't want to see you caught up in some kind of scandal because you have a thing for burlesque or whatever."

Lame, but true. For some reason, he seriously doubted this was some kind of wild side she had hidden over the years. She danced with an innocent honesty, not like a stripper. It was kind of like she was looking for something, an affirmation of some kind. Probably something to do with her fiancé. The papers had been all abuzz when the mayor's daughter had become engaged. Thierry had hated the man instantly. If this woman were his, he would make damn sure all her needs were met. And if she still felt the need to dance half-naked in a room full of strange men, she damned sure wouldn't be doing it without him being front and center.

His hand went from her ear to the back of her neck, pulling her to him.

"Did you drive here?" he asked.

"No," she answered softly. "I took a cab."

Thierry nodded as he stood, holding his hand out to her.

"Let me take you home, sugar. Just to talk, to get to know each other better." Damn, that sounded lame. He wouldn't blame her if she slapped him.

There were a thousand and one reasons for her to end this insanity right now, but she wanted to see where this was going. Never in a million years had she thought she would be attracted to a white man, especially not this man. Nothing good could come of it. Yet, no other man had ever made her feel the thing this man made her feel. Maybe it was all subterfuge, but he looked at her like she was a woman, not as the mayor's daughter or as a Dubois heiress.

Still, she had a nagging fear that he thought she was something she was not.

"Just because I dance here from time to time does not mean I am in the habit of taking strange men home."

Even as she said it, she allowed him to pull her to her feet and into his arms. One hand rubbed her lower back while the other stroked her cheek.

"I never though you were. I would like to get to know you better." *In the Biblical sense.* "Just talk for a while." *And make wild, hot love for the rest of our natural-born lives.* Distracted, he ran his hands through his hair. This was not going well. "Hell, I just want to be near you. I wouldn't blame you if you kneed me in the nuts and ran away. Just give me a chance." Okay, now that was outright begging. It was deflating, but he was willing to try just about anything. Here was his chance to be with the woman of his dreams, and he would do or say anything just to be with her, even if it were just for a little while.

Angelique knew there were hidden meaning behind his words, especially the *"I would like to get to know you better"* bit. She should politely say, "No thank you," and take her ass home, but the words would not come. All her life she had done what was expected of her. Just this once she wanted to take a chance. She could not imagine a worse person to take a chance on, but she found she could not say no. Standing in his arms, she allowed his hands to soothe her misgivings away. Instead of feeling dwarfed by the way he towered over her, she felt protected, and for the first time in her life, cherished. It was a false sentiment surely, but it felt good. God, she wanted to feel this way, if only for a brief time.

Thierry forced himself to take a step back. For a million nights, he had dreamed of this woman in his arms; the reality was almost too much. He wanted to take her right there, on the couch in the dressing room of a high-class strip club, but he couldn't allow his baser urges to overwhelm him. He would do this right even if it killed him—and it just might.

"Come on," he murmured, taking her hand in his. Her hand looked so dainty engulfed in his larger one.

Silently, he followed her down the back stairs and into the parking lot, watching the gentle sway of her hips the entire way. He wanted to reach out and grab those hips and grind then against him. *Easy, boy. We gotta take this slow.*

"My car is over there." Thierry pointed to his car in the corner of the parking lot.

Angelique followed dutifully, sliding in the passenger seat as he held open the door. It was still stupid to go anywhere with him, but at least it wouldn't be boring. He seemed half as nervous as she felt.

"So you usually go to a strip club to find your conquests?" Angelique asked.

"Conquests?" He laughed. "I think you have the wrong idea about me."

"Oh, really? Born to Louisiana's first family, richer than Croesus, you must be a least, what? Thirty? Never been married, and you expect me to believe you haven't have conquests?"

"Nah, I've always been the hunted, not the hunter. And I'm thirty-five, by the way."

She supposed that was true enough. Still, he wasn't exactly the hunted now. He had captured her attention easily enough with little more than a smile and a few choice words. Such a deep, sexy voice with that lazy drawl. He had never sounded like that in any of the interviews she had managed to catch over the years. Or maybe she just hadn't been paying attention.

"So, where are you taking me?" she asked to quiet her wayward thoughts.

"Wait and see, sugar. I just might surprise you."

71

CHAPTER FOUR

As nervous as Angelique had been about getting in the car with Thierry, he drove her straight home. He even opened her car door and walked her to the door.

"Would you like to come in?" she offered awkwardly, not really sure what she would do if he said yes.

He didn't.

"I don't think that would be a good idea right now," he said as he smiled. "I'll call you tomorrow. Maybe we could get together, have lunch or something?"

"Sure." She shrugged, doubting she would ever hear from him again.

She hadn't given him her number, and he hadn't asked. She knew he had waited until she locked the door before walking back to his car; she watched him through the peephole.

She sighed as she watched the morning rays dance across her bed. He had looked back; that meant something, right? Probably not. Thierry Chevalier was way out of her league. She may have come from an old, proud Creole family, but he came from the original settlers of Louisiana. One of the original white, aristocratic Creoles, with roots in this state deeper than a towering cypress. Their kind rarely mixed with others. So what was up with last night?

Never in her wildest dreams had Angelique even entertained the thought of seeing someone like him. Not only would her mother go ballistic, she couldn't imagine what *his* family might think. His father was a freaking United States Senator, and his uncle was some kind of general. Yeah, her father was the mayor, but his family was akin to the Kennedys—only they had been in various parts of the government far longer, and they were twenty times as loaded.

He was incredibly sexy, though. Those aquamarine eyes had seemed to look into her very soul. And those lips! Pure sensuality wrapped in sin. Just a thirty-minute car ride had made her wish for things she could never have. Why had she never noticed how unbelievably delectable he was? *Because you could never have a man like that,* she thought to herself. Men of his type didn't date women of color, not seriously. And good girls from prominent families didn't have sordid affairs. Sighing, she turned over and buried her face in her pillow.

Stop thinking about him; it will never happen.

The blaring ring of the phone brought her out of her ruminations.

"Hello?" Grateful for something to take her mind off the very sexy Thierry Chevalier, she grabbed the phone on the first ring.

There was a brief pause, then the deep, sexy voice came through and made her stomach quiver.

"I didn't wake you, did I?"

Damn, the man sounded good, even over the phone! "No," she breathed, unsure of what to say or how to act.

"Do you have any plans for today?" he asked.

If she did, she would have broken them in that moment. The butterflies in her stomach started to fly around in earnest. What was she thinking? She had just gone over this; he couldn't possibly want her for more than a passing fling, if that. Why the sudden interest in her? Because he'd found her stripping at her friend's club? Someone as well-connected as Thierry had to know who owned the club. As ruthless a businessman as she had heard he was, he had to know she and Katrina were close friends. So what was he driving at?

"Angelique?" he asked, his voice not half as confident as it had been a minute ago.

"Thierry, I don't know what kind of girl you think I am," Angelique began, only to be cut off.

"Stop right there," Thierry's voice came through, every bit as domineering and forceful as she imagined he would be. The mere thought made her insides quiver. Who knew she had a thing for the Alpha-type male?

"I don't *think* anything near what *you* are thinking I do," he informed her.

"No?" she asked skeptically.

"No."

The simple word had come out as some kind of declaration. She melted just a little, waiting to see what he would say next.

"Look," Thierry sighed over the phone. "I just want to see you, spend some time with you. You know, get to know you better."

"And then what?" she asked, afraid of the answer.

"That's up to you, sweetheart," he told her. "I hope we can become...friends."

"Friends, huh?" She couldn't help but sound skeptical. She wanted to get to know him, but she was afraid. Afraid of what he would want from her, and even more afraid of what she might want from him.

"No, not just friends." His voice dipped into a sexy growl, making her heart flutter. " I won't lie to you. I want more—much more. But I don't want a fling, or an affair. I like you."

Simple and to the point; she had to give him that.

"You don't *know* me," she stressed. "How can you say you don't want…those things?"

She heard a heavy sigh on the other end of the phone. "Give me a chance to show you?"

There were a million and one reasons why she shouldn't, but she didn't listen to any of them. If she were going to spend the rest of her life locked in a loveless, passionless marriage, she at least wanted to know what it was like to just once throw caution to the wind and see what happened.

"Okay," she answered simply.

"Okay?" He sounded as if he couldn't believe she'd capitulated. "Really?"

"Yeah, really," she laughed. "What time should I be ready?"

"Just get dressed; I'm already outside."

*****

Thierry had never been so relieved in his life. He liked this woman, *really, really* liked her. On some level, he knew he wouldn't have given up had she said no, but at least he knew she wasn't completely unaffected by him. He wanted this woman in the worst way, but not just for kicks. This was the one woman he wanted to keep forever. He had known for years, but had never really thought through how to talk to her, let alone woo her.

His breath caught when he caught sight of her walking out of her house. He jumped the car, meeting her halfway as she made her way to the curb where his car waited.

"Mornin', sugar," he murmured, giving her a chaste kiss on the cheek.

He let his lips linger, not really touching the smooth softness of her cheek, but inhaling her scent. Clean and fresh, like a bright spring day after a cleansing rain. God, what this woman did to him.

"Um, do I smell okay?" Angelique asked in a low voice, snapping Thierry into the present.

He blushed, quickly straightening to find her smiling at him. Damn, she was beautiful.

"Sorry," he shrugged. "You smell good, nice."

"Clean, even?" she teased, causing his face to enflame even more.

He hadn't blushed since he was a child, but this woman made him feel like an untutored oaf. Not maliciously, like so many women of her status, but in a gentle, teasing kind of way. Just being around her for this short time soothed him in some elemental way. Anyone who thought they knew him would be shocked. Thierry Chevalier was not known to be a soft, sentimental type.

"So, where are we going?" Angelique asked once they were both seated in the car.

"It's a surprise," he told her, smiling.

*****

Angelique could honestly say she had never had a better date. Thierry had taken her out on his boat for the entire afternoon. He had brought a lunch, and they had just kicked back and enjoyed the beauty of the day in the Gulf. She was surprised by the hidden depths Thierry had shown; one would think that. given his privileged position, he would be overbearingly obnoxious. Most of the guys she had known growing up certainly were, and they only had half the money and pedigree he had. He seemed to be a genuinely deep and insightful person. His views on the world surprised her. He was certainly cynical in some ways, but he had an endearing quality to him. He respected people, which was rare for someone of his position in society. Her mother certainly respected no one but those higher on the social ladder than she.

She was sorry when the sun began to set and they headed back. She didn't want the day to end. She couldn't remember the last time she was able to just relax and be herself with someone other than Regina, Jade or Katrina.

"Angel, honey. I know you really don't know me all that well yet," Thierry said, breaking into her thoughts, "but I just don't want this day to end."

It was a line, and she knew it—but she didn't want the day to end either.

"What did you have in mind?" Her heart raced. She had a feeling where this was going. Could she do it?

"I want to show you something. My house, actually."

Just like she'd figured. Even as she questioned her sanity, she found herself agreeing. "Okay, sure."

God, she was ten kinds of fool, but she wanted to see what would happen. What was Thierry after? If it was what she thought it was, would she give in? Looking over at his profile, she was struck again by the sheer masculine beauty of the man. Hell, who was she staying pure for? Paul? It wasn't as if he'd appreciate it. Marriage to him was something that made others happy, something she had been doing her entire life. She was sick to death of doing what was expected of her. Just this once, she would roll the dice and take a chance.

CHAPTER FIVE

Angelique was not at all surprised to find herself in Fauberg Marigny on Pauger Street, not far from her own house. The outside was deceptively simple. From what she could see in the moonlight, the home appeared to be little more than a cottage. Once inside, it was more like a palace. The foyer floors were Italian marble, leading to a formal reception room. The furniture was delicate, all eighteenth-century French colonial. It should have looked too formal to actually use, but it didn't. The sofa and settee were upholstered in a warm tan fabric embroidered with rich red, orange, and green flowers and plants. There were various knick-knacks placed strategically around the room, giving it a lived-in look. At least three gilded frames held paintings of women. Black women.

Angelique whirled to face the man who'd brought her here.

"What, you have some kind of fetish about black women? Is that why you brought me here?"

You knew better, the little voice in her head told her. *This man is a freak*! He probably had some kind of weird fascination with black women in general, *Plaçage* system in general. Maybe it would turn him on to have her as his own personal whore.

"Why don't you go over there and take a closer look, Angel."

It was now or never, Thierry thought to himself. She had to learn about his little obsession sooner or later. If he let go for any amount of time, he might lose her, and he had no intention of ever losing her. He had waited nine years for this woman. The only woman that had moved more than his cock when he thought about her; the woman whose face he saw every time he closed his eyes, no matter whom he was with at the time. There was no way in hell he was going to let her go. Damn all the issues and reasons it was foolish to pursue this particular obsession; Thierry

knew he was walking a tightrope, but he knew in his very

bones this was the woman for him. At her gasp, he gathered

she finally noticed the subject of all three paintings.

"Who painted this?" she demanded in awe, reaching

out to touch the painting before her. It was her. They were

all of her.

"I did."

Angelique jumped. She hadn't realized how close

he was, but he was right behind her. She swallowed hard,

willing herself not to move away, not to show how jittery

he made her feel.

"Why?"

Thierry had to think about that one. Why did his

heart rate quicken and his cock become stiff enough to

drive nails every time he saw her on television or in a

newspaper or magazine? How was it that this woman had

held a deep fascination for him for so long? When he had

seen her on stage, he had wanted to carve the eyes out of every person in that room, then take her right there and make her his forever. She would be his; she just needed to come to that conclusion herself.

"Because you're beautiful." He leaned forward to whisper in her ear. "And you make me feel things I never felt for any other person. Because you are you, Angel."

Angelique found she could not respond. What could she say? It was beyond a little weird that Thierry Chevalier had portraits of her hanging in his living room, ones he had painted himself, no less. If this was some sort of set up, he had put an awful lot into it. This was beginning to get way too complicated. She'd agreed to come with him to see what would happen. A part of her had expected some sort of ambush; many scenarios had run through her mind, including local television reporters shoving cameras in her face and asking her why she was moonlighting as a stripper, or a detailed seduction with someone "accidentally" walking in. She had expected to be taken to the condo the entire city knew he kept at The Pontalba, where many a nubile blonde or redhead—sources said they were all he dated—had been rumored to disappear through his front door, not to reemerge for the rest of the night. With the exception of tourists, there wasn't a soul in the Big Easy who hadn't heard rumors of his exploits and prowess. Yeah, she had been a little more than curious to see where this would lead.

"Let me show you the rest of the house," Thierry offered, ushering her from the room.

He showed her the kitchen that could only be described as a master chef's wettest dream, complete with a refurbished nineteenth-century carpenter's table that served as an island. There was even a wine closet located in the back corner. From there they went to the music room complete with grand piano and an antique harpsichord, through a small enclosed courtyard complete with garden, back inside to what looked like the informal living room. Thierry ushered her to a large suede sofa, seating himself by her side.

"You have a lovely home," she offered, feeling more and more unsure of herself. His eyes never left her as she squirmed in her seat. "Do you live here now? I mean, I thought you lived at The Pontalba."

"I just finished refurbishing this place," Thierry explained. "I still have my apartment, though. This place is a little big for just me."

Okaaay, was that a hint? Of course not! Even if he did mean that he was ready to settle down, she was engaged. Just the thought was beginning to make her a little sick to her stomach.

"Why did you bring me here?" Angelique blurted out before she lost her nerve. Straightforward and to the point was definitely not one of her finer qualities. It was past time she learned how to be both.

Thierry lay back and pondered the question. He hadn't really thought beyond getting her here. Well, that wasn't true, but he couldn't very well tell her he wanted to make love to her six ways to Sunday until he was the only man she could ever imagine between those luscious thighs. He decided to ignore the question entirely and throw a hardball her way.

"Do you love your fiancé?"

Her head jerked up so fast he thought she would get whiplash.

"What?"

He leaned closer, gratified she didn't move back.

"You know, sugar. Paul Guidry: about six-foot-two; one hundred seventy-five, one hundred eighty pounds; Wharton School graduate. Ring a bell?"

He watched as she swallowed hard, chewing her lower lip. Nope, she didn't love Mr. Wanna-Be-Playboy, but she had no idea how to answer his question. Excellent.

"Look, I should be going." She jumped to her feet.

Thierry rose and stepped closer, reaching out to push a wayward curl behind her ear.

"You didn't answer my question." He leaned down until their lips were just a whisper apart. "Well, do you?"

Angelique watched his mouth, transfixed. He had beautiful lips, full and kissable. They looked so soft, they looked like they were…

All thought abruptly ceased as their lips met. He didn't take it slow. He dominated her with this kiss. His tongue invaded her mouth as he dug one hand in her hair, forcing her head back, while the other pulled her flush against him. A helpless moan escaped as his mouth moved against hers, nipping her upper lip, then the lower one before moving to her chin, her cheek, her neck. The hand at her back moved up and down her spine, stopping at her ass. The other hand released the firm grip he had on her hair to join its counterpart, grinding her suddenly weeping center into his rigid member.

"Stay with me," Thierry whispered in her ear, lightly biting her earlobe.

Angelique nodded her head before she thought better of it. In a heartbeat, he swept her up into his arms, carrying her up the staircase into the bedroom. The tour hadn't included the upper rooms. The master bedroom looked like some kind of bohemian dream, a combination of Indian and Moroccan harem. The only modern convenience was the huge mahogany four-post platform bed. She gulped. He probably wasn't expecting an unschooled virgin in that bed tonight. Oh God, what was she doing? She had to stop this now, before it went too far to pull back.

Why stop it? The naughty little voice inside her asked. *For Paul? For your mother? What about what you want?* What did she want? As Thierry devoured her lips once more, she knew. She wanted him in a way she had never wanted anyone. She allowed him to pull her t-shirt up and over her head, then hook into the waistband of the sweatpants. She closed her eyes as he bent, lowering her pants, lifting first one foot then the other to pull them completely off. Had she taken off her own shoes? She couldn't remember. She didn't want to open her eyes to see herself standing in her underwear and her socks.

"Damn, you're beautiful."

Angelique jumped at the rough voice so close to her ear. Her head tilted of its own accord at the feel of lips on the side of her neck. God, it was so good to feel his hot mouth biting and kissing the side of her neck! His arms encircled her waist, pulling her back against him. When had he taken off his shirt? She wanted to turn around to see the hard muscles she felt against her back, but his hold was firm. She could feel him against her ass through his pants.

It couldn't be as big as it felt, could it? He cupped her breasts, his mouth moving back to her ear.

"I've wanted this for so long," he rasped, and for the first time she believed him. "Wanted you for so damn long."

A woman could get a swelled head at the raw need she heard in his voice, felt in his touch. It seemed to take forever for him to take her panties off. She shivered, though she was anything but cold. She had never been naked in front of another human being since she was a child. From his groan, she supposed he approved. All too soon she was lying on the satin coverlet, spread out like a feast. His eyes roamed over her as if he was trying to memorize every curve. She had never felt so vulnerable in all her life. His eyes widened as they found her waxed vagina.

"Oh, baby," Thierry whispered, caressing what had to be the prettiest pussy he had ever seen.

She was so much more than he had ever dreamed. Her skin was softer than he had imagined, and her body curved delightfully in all the right places, offering comfort and succor to his barren soul. His fingers skimmed the outer lips of her bare vagina, lightly pulling on her clitoris. Angelique moaned, arching her hips, her legs opening wider of their own accord. His hand became bolder, dipping into the part of her that had never felt so empty before, retreating to massage her awakening nub, then back down to start the process all over again.

She tried not to moan, not to beg, but the broken "*please*," followed by pants and cries, could not be kept inside. Never in her darkened bedroom, fantasizing about a phantom lover, had she ever felt the longing and desire she experienced right now. It seemed as though his fingers knew her body better than she ever could, driving her higher and higher to some unknown summit. His sparkling eyes seemed to radiate a greenish-blue fire that never left her face. She should feel mortified being completely nude and on display, but she couldn't feel anything beyond the magic of his caress. When his one finger became two, stroking inside her with such exquisite expertise, Angelique felt herself falling completely apart, flying to a zenith never reached by her own pitiful attempts at self-gratification.

"That's it, sugar. Come for me."

With a strangled cry, she did just that. Her body spasmed as his thumb circled her clit and his fingers pressed deeper inside her. Thierry felt like he would come along with her; never had he seen a more magnificent sight than Angelique Dubois coming by his hand. Before she had a chance to recover, he dropped to his knees, his hands cupping her buttocks to bring her to his waiting mouth. He closed his mouth as the taste of her burst on his tongue. Fuck ambrosia, this was truly the nectar of the gods! She was like Mexican chocolate, hot, sweet, and spicy. How the hell had he lived as long as he had without this woman? He thrust his tongue as deep as it would go before moving back to lap at the juices that threatened to escape. Like a starving man, he drank every drop, then demanded more. He had lost count of how often he drove her over the edge, but it wasn't enough.

Angelique was dying. You could die from pleasure, couldn't you? It seemed that just as she was descending from one peak, he was pushing her back up the mountain again. Strangely, the only thought in her scattered mind was an odd line out of a T.S. Eliot poem: *"Asleep . . . tired . . . or it malingers, / Stretched on the floor, here beside you and me. / Should I, after tea and cakes and ices, / Have the strength to force the moment to its crisis?"* Just when she knew her heart would surely give out, he rose to his feet, as naked as he came into the world.

No baby had ever looked like that. He was magnificent, all hard and sinewy muscle. When she dared glance below his waist, she gasped. No, that couldn't be right. There was no way he was planning on sticking that inside her, was he? Granted, she had never actually seen a penis up close and personal, but that thing looked like a battering ram! It stood out proud, red, and furious, with pearly drops of fluid escaping from its one eye. What was left of her rational mind screamed "Run!"—but her body was not listening. His eyes held her captive as he laid that gorgeous body on top of her. *Oh God, it's really going to happen!* she thought as she felt him probe her opening. Not only happening, but happening with Thierry Chevalier, of all people. Surely she would die and they would find her here, naked, split apart from a massive tool she had no business trying to accommodate. Yep, tabloid fodder for weeks. She braced herself as much as she could when she felt him slide inside. Then he was gone.

Thierry jerked his hips away just in the nick of time. Surely he hadn't just felt what he thought he did.

"Angel, baby, are you . . . have you ever been with a man before?" he managed to ask softly. His heart was racing, his penis throbbing, practically crying at the denial of its one true home.

"Um, no."

Her voice was so low he could barely hear her, but his cock certainly had; he felt like he was about to burst his skin, he wanted her so damn bad. His mind struggled to grip the thought. Never touched before, and all his. As much as he wanted to stake his claim irrevocably, he knew he would have to take it slow. Would she be on the pill? There was no way in hell he was going wear a condom for this; he had to feel her, had to make sure his seed implanted itself deep in her belly, even if she didn't conceive. The need was primitive, but he was far too gone to give a damn. This was his woman, and he would make damn sure of that.

"Sugar, are you on the pill?"

Shit! How could she be so stupid? She had a prescription she had never bothered to fill. There didn't seem to a point. And now here she was, sprawled like some kind of hussy underneath one of the most gorgeous men in all of Louisiana—hell, in the entire country—feeling like an idiot.

"Let me up," she muttered, pushing unsuccessfully against his chest.

Thierry couldn't help but smile. She was embarrassed. Still, she was not about to walk out on him.

"Relax, baby," he soothed, stroking her cheek but refusing to budge. "Honey, I just don't want to regret this." He waited until she stopped squirming, trying to get away.

"Don't you have condoms?" she asked after unsuccessfully trying to wiggle her way free. "I mean, we should be using them anyway. I really don't know you all that well . . ." She didn't know him at all, which made what she had been about to do twice as unbelievable.

He did, but he wasn't about to tell her that. He wasn't going to take her now, not like this. Her first time would be special; he would make damn sure of that. He had become sexually active at the ripe old age of fifteen, and from that moment until now, he had never slept with any woman without protection. Now that he knew she had never slept with anyone at all, he made a mental note to throw his condoms out. There would never be another woman for him, and he would do everything within his power—and maybe some things outside of it—to make sure she never had to look to anyone but him for her every need.

He settled himself in bed, pulling her close, wrapping her in his arms, and throwing a leg over hers for good measure.

"Relax, sugar," he murmured. "I can wait."

Wait? Did he expect a repeat performance? Okay, granted, she hadn't done much but come and come some more. He sounded—permanent. No, surely it was just her imagination. She would simply wait until he fell asleep, then sneak out and pretend this never happened.

CHAPTER SIX

Thierry woke with the first rays of the sun streaking across the sky. Snuggling close to the delectable little bundle tucked against his side, he let his thoughts go over the events of the past forty-eight hours. When he'd gotten out of bed the day before yesterday, he'd been involved in a meaningless sexual relationship with a grasping golddigger, had a career he hated, and was trapped in a never-ending cycle of family obligations. True, not that much had changed yet, but now that he'd finally met Angelique, had finally gotten to touch her, hold her, kiss her, he was determined to change everything.

The problem was not with his family; his cousins would be there no matter what, and truthfully, they were the only ones he gave a damn about. The problem would be Angelique. She obviously felt something for him; if she hadn't, they wouldn't have come so close to making love. You didn't keep your virginity for twenty-five years to just give it up to anyone. He had felt the way her pulse quickened when he kissed her; he had tasted the evidence of her longing. She was obviously confused, and who could blame her? He hadn't exactly been subtle. Twice she had attempted to slip out of the bed when she thought he was asleep. Hell, he didn't blame her for that either. Those paintings in the parlor couldn't have helped. What kind of guy paints a woman he doesn't know, then strong-arms her into coming home with him? He grimaced as he saw himself the way she must have. Stalker.

Carefully slipping from the bed, Thierry went into the restroom for a quick shower before making his way to the kitchen. He wanted to serve her breakfast in bed, catch her off-guard before she had a chance to come up with reasons why she should leave. Not until he actually opened the empty refrigerator did he remember he didn't have any real food in the house, plus he couldn't cook.

Mumbling expletives, he quietly made his way back to the bedroom to dig his cell out of his pants. Looking down at the piles of clothes on the floor, he smiled wickedly before scooping them all up and heading back downstairs. If she were to wake up, she would have a hard time sneaking out without a stitch to wear. It was playing dirty, but he was playing for keeps. There was no way she wouldn't be more than a little upset waking up in his bed in the cold light of day. It was important to get her to know him, to see that he wasn't out for a cheap thrill. If that meant keeping her here for a little while, so be it.

He chuckled at his own cleverness as he deposited her jeans and t-shirt in the washing machine. He didn't have any detergent, but he turned it on anyway and went back into the kitchen to call Remy. Remy could cook and probably hadn't made it to bed yet. He would just get him to drop something off and get rid of him before Angelique woke.

"Why in the name of all that's holy are you calling me at such a God forsaken hour?" Remy answered after his second attempt at reaching him.

"I need a favor."

The line was quiet for so long, Thierry was afraid Remy had hung up.

"Remy?"

"Yeah," came the muffled reply. "This is Thierry, right?"

"Yes, it's me," he answered impatiently. "And I really need you to do something for me, Remy."

"Have you been arrested?" Remy demanded. "Did that stripper mug you or something?"

"What?"

"Well, the Thierry I know has never asked me for anything, so the best I can come up with is either you've been arrested, or the stripper you took off with the night before last knocked you upside your head and stole all your worldly possessions."

"She wasn't a stripper," Thierry angrily retorted before he thought better of it.

"Uh-huh. Let me guess," came the sarcastic reply, "working her way through college?"

"Look, stop being an ass! I need you to, uh, cook breakfast for me." God, he felt like a fool. He was really going to have to learn how to cook.

"Excuse me?"

"Look Remy, I wanted to . . ." Damn, how was he going to phrase this so it didn't sound as ridiculous as he felt? "I have a guest . . ."

"You don't say." Despite the fact it was barely eight o'clock in the morning, Remy was really starting to enjoy himself.

"Can you do it or not?" Thierry growled into the phone.

Remy was hard-pressed not to crack up. This was too good. "Can I do what?"

"Cook breakfast—for two."

"I'll be down in two shakes," Remy told him, sitting up in bed and rubbing his hands together. He lived in the floor above his cousin at their famous residence, so when he had finally gotten in last night around three, he had stopped by Thierry's only to find that Thierry wasn't there. Using the spare key his cousin had given him, he had entered the place. From the look of it, Thierry hadn't been there since leaving for the Kat's Meow. He had to see the woman who had kept his straight-laced cousin out so late, and then stayed the night. Thierry rarely brought women home, and one staying the night might not be unheard of, but he never let them stay long enough for breakfast. He had always said it gave them ideas.

"I, uh, I'm not at the apartment," Thierry mumbled.

Remy didn't bother to hold in his laughter this time.

"Well, where the hell are you, boy? How the hell can I come cook if I don't know where you are?"

Regretting it, but not having a lot of options, Thierry gave Remy the address and quick directions.

"And Remy," he added, "cook there and just drop off the food."

He wasn't really sure Remy heard the last part, since his cousin hung up rather quickly; but thirty minutes later, when he went to answer the pounding at the door, he knew he hadn't.

Remy stood there with three large shopping backs and a wicked grin.

"Where's the kitchen?" Remy asked, walking right past him without missing a beat.

"Can you keep it down?" Thierry hissed, thankful he had closed the bedroom door after he laid out toiletries

and one of his shirts for Angelique. "This way. And I told
you to cook at home and just drop off the food!"

From look on Remy's face, Thierry revised his
earlier opinion. He had heard Thierry and just ignored him.

"Couldn't do that," Remy said, digging into the
bags—"wouldn't be fresh." He looked up, still sporting that
damnable shit-eating grin. "So how was your first night
with a stripper? And a black one at that! What would Lady
Rienne say?"

Thierry clenched his jaw as he fought the urge to
punch his playboy cousin in the face, regretting the fact that
he couldn't hit him yet; he had to wait until he was done
cooking. Then he could kick Remy's ass.

"For the last time," Thierry warned, "she is not a
stripper. And I don't give a damn what Lady Rienne thinks
about anything."

"Riiiiiight," Remy answered, not in the least
chastened, before he turned and began to work his magic.

Not many people knew Remy was a gourmet. He made damn sure most people thought of him as nothing more than a reprobate lady's man who drank and whored his life away. On the surface it looked like he was rebelling against the strict upbringing of Lady Rienne, who ran her household with military discipline and expected absolute obedience. All of her grandsons had gone on to careers she had decided they should have—all except Remy. She had been horrified when the seventeen-year-old high school graduate wanted to attend culinary school. Nothing was more important to her than the family name and appearances. A Chevalier could not be a chef. So Remy had been promptly shipped off to Yale, where he studied business. She had wanted him to work with Thierry. Remy complied with her wishes until he graduated from grad school, but when he returned home, he seemed bound and determined to defy the old lady at every turn. He refused to work, and thanks to the trust fund managed by Thierry, he didn't have to.

Lady Rienne had tried to talk Thierry into cutting Remy off until he toed the line, but Thierry had long since been done with taking orders from the woman he despised. Most grandmothers were warm and loving; Lady Rienne was a dragon. The only reason Thierry headed the family's vast holdings was to find a way to be independent of her domineering ways. He controlled the money, so he was able to set up quite a nice nest egg for himself and his cousins that she couldn't touch. That was the only reason he stayed LeBlanc, Inc.: he was biding his time, waiting for his real life to begin. Hopefully, last night was the start of that life.

"If you are done daydreaming, your breakfast is just about ready."

Remy's voice brought Thierry out of his ruminations. *Damn!* he thought, scrubbing his hands across his face. *One night with the woman, and I'm getting all soft and thoughtful.*

"Okay, Remy," Thierry said, taking the other man's arms in a firm grip to escort him out of the kitchen towards the front door. "Thanks for coming."

But Remy was no longer moving. He stopped, looking up towards the staircase that curved down into the parlor. Thierry cursed under his breath before turning his eyes upward, knowing what he would see.   Angelique stood in the middle of the staircase. Her damp hair was drawn up in tight ringlets that fell to the middle of her back, her provocative curves were barely hidden by his tailored dress shirt that brushed the top of her knees, and her little white teeth were worrying her lower lip. Thierry groaned in spite of himself. How could anyone look so deliciously sweet yet devilishly enchanting at the same time?

"That's not the stripper from the other night," Remy declared, gawking at the woman on the stairs. "That's . . ."

"Yeah, I know who it is," Thierry mumbled, trying to push Remy towards the door.

Remy wasn't budging.

"Well hello, sweetness," Remy drawled merrily, walking to the foot of the staircase and leaning against the intricately carved banister. "I'm Remy."

The little bastard was holding his hand out as if to assist her the rest of the way down. Thierry had to elbow him in the stomach to make him move.

"Who is just leaving," he said, shoving his cousin back towards the door. Remy quickly stepped around him.

"After I meet this delightful vision of loveliness," Remy assured him with a even bigger smile.

Angelique stood frozen, clutching the railing as if it were a lifeline. She had woken up in the bed of Thierry-freaking-Chevalier only to find that her clothes had disappeared; then, after getting the courage to leave the room, she ran smack dab into the biggest male whore in entire South. Coupled with her complete mortification over what happened last night, this day couldn't get any worse. She blinked in surprise as she felt very strong hands prying hers away from the only thing keeping her upright. Thierry was frowning down at her, urging her down the stairs.

"Are you okay?" he whispered for her ears alone. Unfortunately, Remy had excellent hearing.

"Why wouldn't she be okay?" he asked, stepping up to them as they reached the main floor. "Did this mean man hurt you, sweetheart?"

Angelique couldn't help thinking this situation would be funny had it happened to anyone else. Remy was obviously working hard to get a rise out of Thierry, and it appeared to be working. Once again, doubts about his motives flashed into her mind. Why was Remy really here? What did they want from her?

"Look, I just want my clothes." Angelique spoke up for the first time. "Then I'll be on my way."

"Now, sweetheart, you can't run off before tasting the feast I cooked just for you," Remy coaxed, reaching out to take hold of her hand, only to find his own hand intercepted by a very furious-looking Thierry.

Well, now that was interesting. Remy had grown up with Thierry, and never had he seen him look as mad and possessive as he did right now. At a momentary loss for words, Remy looked at the woman once more. She seemed to be familiar, but he couldn't quite place her. She could have been the stripper from the night before, but the stripper had worn a mask and had straighter hair. He let his eyes wander down to take in her petite figure, only to have Thierry wrap his arms around her, effectively shielding most of her body from his view. Oh, this was getting better than he'd ever dreamed.

"Leave now, Remy, or I might have to hurt you."

Remy looked in shock at the man he thought he knew. Dear God, Thierry had it bad! Remy had heard the expression spittin' mad, but he had never really seen it until now. The man reputed to have ice water running through his veins actually looked like he was about to do him some serious damage. Taking a quick glance back at the woman, he could see her dark face turn deep rose from embarrassment. She was looking intently at her feet, but her body had unconsciously melded back against Thierry's bigger, harder frame. Lady Rienne was going to have a heart attack. Thierry was in love, deeply from the looks of it. And if he knew his cousin, nothing was going to make him let her go.

"Well, my work here is done for now." Remy sounded a great deal less amused than he had a few minutes earlier. He turned and got halfway to the door before turning around once more. "I'll be by around one with lunch." With a sad smile he walked out, closing the heavy oak door quietly behind him.

As soon as Remy closed the door, all the anger Thierry had had a hard time controlling drained from his body. Though she had no idea she was doing it, Angelique had relaxed her body against his as if seeking protection. Not giving her time to realize she was once again wrapped in his arms, he turned her around. Taking advantage of her lips slightly agape, he kissed her thoroughly until she was moaning softly against his lips. God, she tasted so good! He had to force himself to take a step back, still holding her so she couldn't escape.

"Good morning, Angel."

Angelique was more confused than she had ever been. She had come downstairs with every intention of finding her clothes and taking her ass home, but one kiss and she was a quivering mass of need. Why the hell couldn't Paul make her feel like this? Why the hell didn't he want to?

"Let's eat in the garden, shall we?" Thierry went on, like the entire episode with Remy had never happened.

She let him lead her out to the small enclosed garden right outside of the kitchen, where he sat her on one of the black wrought-iron chairs. As soon as she was seated, he went back inside to collect the food. She watched him disappear through the sliding glass door before she sank her head in her hands. Deciding to go dance last night was either the worst mistake she had ever made in her life or the best thing that had ever happened to her. She wished she knew which. Yesterday she might have been miserable, but she hadn't been confused. The one thing she knew for sure was there was no way she could marry Paul. Not that she could ever have anything serious with Thierry, but now that she knew what passion felt like, she wouldn't be satisfied with a cold marriage for anyone's sake. Her

mother would likely be furious, but she wanted just a little

of what Thierry had shown her when she did find the right

guy. She would also have to start taking birth control. Not

that she would get carried away and actually sleep with

someone without a condom. She couldn't believe she had

come so close last night. If he hadn't stopped . . .

But he had stopped. Not only had he asked

nothing more of her, he had held her tight throughout the

night. When she thought he had drifted off to sleep, she had

attempted to ease out of the bed, only to have him drag her

back into his embrace not once, but twice. She just didn't

get it. What the hell was he after? She'd heard Remy ask if

she was the stripper last night, and she'd heard his answer.

It was obvious Remy had no idea who she was, and Thierry

hadn't bothered to enlighten him. Why? Was he waiting

until later? But then, his anger at his cousin not leaving had

been very real. She had been terrified he might actually

punch the other man. And she had just stood there like an idiot.

"Here you go, sweetheart."

Breakfast consisted of Eggs Orleans, roasted home fries, fresh fruit, blueberry scones, and fresh-squeezed orange juice. They ate in compatible silence for a few minutes before Angelique worked up her nerve to ask him the question burning in her mind.

"Thierry, what do you want from me? I mean, really?"

He leaned back in his chair to look at her. He was quiet so long she wondered if he would answer. Angelique squirmed in her seat, made uncomfortable by his scrutiny.

"What do you think I want from you, Angel?" he finally asked, his voice barely above a whisper, making her shiver with need.

"I don't know!" she cried, shoving her half-full plate away. "How am I supposed to know? You drag me here . . . Okay, maybe you didn't drag me here, but what was I supposed to think? You knew who I was! I was afraid you might say something or do something. Look, I don't know what you're thinking. In fact, I don't know anything about you! This whole thing is bizarre, to say the least. So, why am I here? What do you want? And why the hell have you been painting my portrait, anyway?"

With her chest heaving, her eyes blazing, and her tight corkscrew curls in a wild disarray, Angelique was the most breathtaking woman Thierry had ever seen in his life. His heart expanded in his chest, confirming what he had known when he first saw her years ago. He loved her. Madly, desperately. This was the woman he wanted by his side for the rest of his life. Standing, he pulled her up into his arms.

"You, Angel," he told her firmly. "All I want is you."

CHAPTER SEVEN

The first thing Angelique did when she returned home on Monday was call Regina. She had spent the entire weekend with Thierry in his elegant cottage, slept next to him in his bed, but they hadn't had sex. Nor had there been a repeat of the intense foreplay of the first night. She should have felt relieved he hadn't asked anything from her except to pose for him in the garden wearing nothing but his dress shirt. How could she say no? But instead of being grateful he hadn't tried anything, she just felt frustrated. She didn't understand what he wanted from her, but she had to admit, she really liked Thierry. He was nothing like any of the stories she had heard. They had spent the majority of the weekend lying around, just talking. They'd talked about their childhood, their dreams, their respective families. Who knew Thierry Chevalier had wanted nothing more than to be a painter when he was growing up? He obviously hated his choice of career, though it fascinated Angelique.

She had wanted to go into the family business, but her mother was having none of that. As usual, Angelique had acquiesced.

She had told Thierry of her desire to get into some sort of business, and instead of patting her on the head and telling her all the reasons why she shouldn't, he had thought she should go for it.

"Why don't you do it?" he'd asked while playing with her hair.

Angelique had just shrugged. Her mother would never let her hear the end of it if she went to work, and her father would never let her work for him as long as it made her mother unhappy. She couldn't really say her parents had a loving relationship; they were rarely in the same place at the same time, and when they were, her mother provided the bulk of the discourse. It was more like her father wouldn't want to hear the endless grief he'd get from her mother if he gave his daughter a job. She could

technically use her inheritance to start her own business.
She had given the idea some serious thought lately, but she
wasn't brave enough to face the wraith of Charline Dubois.
She had thought to wait until after her marriage. But now
that marriage wasn't going to happen.

It was weird, but Thierry seemed to know exactly
what was running through her mind.

"Why do you let people tell you what you can't
do?" he had asked her.

"I do not," she had defended. "Maybe I'm just not
ready yet."

Thierry had sat up from where they were
sprawled on the floor, taking her along with him. Holding
her chin firmly to make sure he had her full attention, he
spoke clearly and concisely.

"You are a quick, intelligent woman with the
heart of a lion, if you would just learn to trust yourself."

Yeah, right. She had tried to look away, but he hadn't been about to let her slip into old self-doubts.

"Sugar, whether or not you had on a mask, it takes a hell of a lot of guts to get up on a stage in front a bunch of horny men and dance like you're the only one in the room. I damn sure couldn't do it."

She had really never thought of it like that. For her, it was an undercover form of rebellion or a release of all things she wished she could do. He made her feel like she really could do anything.

This was getting a little too deep. She was completely out of her element. Never once had she met a man who was interested in what she wanted, or who cared whether or not she followed her heart. But there was no way she could see him again. If news got out, all hell would surely break loose. It may the twenty-first century in California or New York, but this was still the good old

South. With both of their families being so much in the public eye, it would cause nothing but grief on both sides.

Sighing, she dialed Regina.

"Hey, girl! What's up?" Regina's bubbly voice answered on the first ring. "What happened to you yesterday?"

Damn! They were all supposed to meet for brunch, but Angelique had completely forgotten.

"I'm sorry, it just slipped my mind," she hedged.

Actually, she had been lounging in bed with Thierry while Remy was downstairs making the best brunch she'd ever had in her life. Remy had come to cook periodically throughout the weekend, silently coming and going, leaving the most scrumptious treats as the only clue he had ever been there. There had been quiche florentine, ham-and-cheese strata, sweet-potato hash browns, grilled asparagus and prosciutto salad, fresh strawberries with coconut crème Anglaise, and mimosas. Remy had turned

out to be a damn good cook.

"Sollie was hoppin' mad. I think she must have

gone by your house five times. I know she called your

mother at least twice."

Shit! She was in for it now. She had to think

about a plausible excuse for her to be gone all weekend

without calling anyone.

"Yeah, well, that's kind of what I want to talk to

you about," Angelique said.

"Sure, shoot."

"Um, I'd rather come by your office a little later.

If you have the time."

There were sounds of papers rustling for a few

minutes. Leave it to Regina to be in the office before eight

on a Monday morning.

"How about ten?"

"That would be great." Angelique breathed a sigh of relief. She could talk to any of her friends, really, with the exception of Solange, but Regina was more even-headed than most. She was always good for impartial advice without bringing in any of her own hang-ups.

Putting all her doubts and fears about Thierry on the back burner for the time being, Angelique took a leisurely shower and went about grooming herself for the day ahead while thinking of ways to break up with Paul. Truthfully, she should never have agreed to marry him in the first place, but she'd allowed her mother to pressure her into something she hadn't wanted yet again. It really had to stop. Although he hadn't said anything outright, over the past weekend Thierry had opened her eyes to the fact she'd let her mother run her life in every respect for far too long. She would never be happy living for someone else. Maybe Charline was as controlling as she was because she loved her daughter and didn't want Angelique to make mistakes that would leave her heartbroken or worse. But as much as she would like to believe that, Angelique doubted it. Her mother had never been one to show any kind of affection unless someone was around to witness it. As a child, she'd often gotten the feeling her mother didn't like her much at all, maybe even resented her. All her life Angelique had tried being obedient, following Charline's every dictate to earn her approval and maybe even her love. It had not been effective thus far. Angelique could see now that it was probably never going to happen.

Hours later, as she sat beside Regina on the couch, Angelique came to the epiphany her friends had been waiting for since they'd really gotten to know her well.

"I will never make her happy," she whispered after she'd recounted the entire weekend and all the jumbled emotions her time with Thierry had caused. "Even if I married Paul, she wouldn't be satisfied. There would always be something, wouldn't there?"

The question was completely rhetorical, so Regina didn't bother answering.

"So why shouldn't I see what the thing is with this guy?" Angelique continued, getting to her feet and pacing the office. "I can't keep living my life for my mother, or some archaic sense of family honor, right?" Swinging around to face Regina, she continued, hands akimbo. "And I am sick and tired of being the sweet one, the one that always does the right thing. What the hell has that gotten me? I am a twenty-five-year-old virgin engaged to a man I barely know, and I'm not sure I even like the whoring snake!"

Watching Angelique standing there, glaring at her like she was the one oppressing her, Regina had to smile. Finally, the backbone she'd always known was there was emerging, and all it took to bring it out was a weekend with a strange man. Who knew? Still, what Angelique had done this weekend was extremely dangerous. She hadn't told her who this man was, and Regina feared the worst. Sure, he may not have tried anything yet, but maybe he was just setting her friend up for a bigger scam or fall from grace. There were plenty of people in New Orleans who would like nothing better than to see the Angelic Angelique take a momentous tumble from her pedestal as the sweet, innocent daughter of the beloved mayor. People could be really sick sometimes.

"So, are you going to see this guy again?" Regina asked casually. Years of experience had taught her it was best not to be too forward. That would only serve to make Angelique defensive and, as a result, she would be less than forthcoming.

Angelique sighed as she plopped down on the couch once more. "I don't know. I mean, I want to. I really, really want to. But Thierry is from a completely different world, you know? Plus, I can't imagine his family would be happy were we to have an actual relationship. Not to mention what it could do to Daddy's career."

"Thierry?" Regina prodded gently. "Well, from what you told me, he seems to be pretty into you. I just want you to be careful with someone you don't know. Especially some guy you met at one of Katrina's clubs. You don't know this guy from Adam."

"Oh, I know about him well enough." Angelique answered, distracted by thoughts of her weekend with the enigmatic Thierry. Completely forgetting where she was, she began to reason it all out as if talking to herself. "I have never had anyone look at me like that. I mean, I have always wanted that, you know. Someone to look at me like I were the only woman on earth, like I were the most beautiful thing he had ever seen." Jumping up again, she resumed pacing. "It was weird. He knew who I was even with a mask on. Then, when he took me to his house, he had all these paintings of me. It should have freaked me

out, but it didn't."

"Paintings of you?" Regina interjected.

"Yeah." Angelique waved her friend off and

resumed her diatribe. "He's been painting me since I was,

like, sixteen. They're all over the place, in the living room,

in the den. I even sat for him so he could sketch me. He

wanted to know me. Like, really know me. He listened to

me like you or Katrina would. And he didn't ask me, you

know, to reciprocate when we . . . when he . . . well, he

soothed me and asked for nothing in return. He just asked

me to get on the pill as soon as possible."

"Wait, Angel, stop," Regina demanded, now on

her feet. "What do you mean *soothed you*?"

Angelique felt heat rush to her face. "He, uh,

touched me and stuff."

"Jesus, girl, you can say it," Regina ran blew out

an exasperated breath. "You're an adult."

"He went down on me, okay? A few times. I just can't figure Thierry Chevalier out…"

Regina fell back on the couch as if punched. "Did you say Thierry Chevalier? Angel, girl, I think you need start from the beginning."

*****

Thierry didn't go back to the house after dropping Angelique off at home. He didn't think he could be in the place without seeing Angelique everywhere he looked. Damn, but the woman was sweet. He'd been rock hard all weekend without release. Shifting uncomfortably behind the wheel, all he could think of was the taste of her skin, the way she gasped whenever he touched her, the way she bit her bottom lip right before she came. Groaning, he tried to force his thoughts on his plans for the day. The first thing he needed to do was have a little talk with Miss Katrina Smith. Though she was under no obligation to inform him of Angelique's activities, she definitely needed to be more diligent about whom she hired, especially where his woman was concerned. And Angelique was definitely his woman, even if she hadn't realized it yet. He couldn't imagine being with another woman after this weekend. Unfortunately, that meant he was going to have to satisfy himself for the foreseeable future.

Not that she hadn't offered. Thierry smiled at the memory of her shy offer. He had wanted to say yes with every fiber of his being. To see those edible lips wrapped around him would surely have been the most erotic sight in the world. But he wanted her to trust him first. He needed her to see he wasn't just trying to get off, but wanted something deeper. He wanted her heart.

Letting himself into his apartment, he growled at the sight of Remy curled up on his couch.

"Get up and get out," Thierry snarled, kicking his cousin's boot-clad feet off the Italian leather.

Remy sat up slowly, rubbing the sleep from his eyes.

"Hey, what time is it?"

"It's time for you to go home," Thierry replied, walking into his bedroom.

Completely unabashed, Remy followed him, looking like he had been up all night. He probably had, the reprobate.

"So?" Remy asked, leaning against the bedroom door.

"So, what?"

"Is it serious or what?" Remy demanded.

Thierry wasn't so sure he was ready to share what he'd found in Angelique with anyone, even the cousins he loved like brothers. Still, Remy had no doubt seen too much to try to bullshit him.

"What do you think?" he answered, evading the question.

Remy studied him for a few minutes, seeing far too much in Thierry's estimation.

"I think you need to tread carefully, especially where our grandmother is concerned," Remy said quietly.

"Shit, Remy, I am not living my life for that bitter old . . ." Thierry stopped, exhaling harshly. "Look, I know Lady Rienne is going to be a problem, but I will not allow her to stand in my way."

"Good." Remy nodded, then turned and left, leaving Thierry to shake his head in wonder. Anyone who wrote his cousin off as just an over-privileged playboy was seriously underestimating him.

After laying out his clothes for the day, Thierry went to take a long cold shower. Looking down, he tried to will his erection away, to no avail. It would help if his mind could stop wandering back to the way Angelique looked stretched out on his bed. He had never seen anything as sweet as the way her thighs opened for him, or that

137

beautifully waxed pussy. And the way she tasted . . . He

didn't even realized he had grasped himself until he heard

his own unmistakable moan echo off the bathroom walls.

Stroking himself, his mind went over every curve of her

delectable body. She was round and soft in all the right

places. She was sweet innocence and raw sexuality all

rolled up in one. His mouth began to water remembering

the way her nipple hardened for his questing mouth, the

way her body shuddered in his direction. Stroking faster, he

recalled the way her back arched off the mattress when he

licked and sucked until she was screaming. He erupted at

the last thought, finally feeling the icy pelt of water raining

down on him. With a wry smile, he adjusted the

temperature. He wondered how long he'd be able to hold

out with the temptation of the perfect woman, sleeping

cuddled next to him every night—because there was no

way in hell he'd spend another night without her.

CHAPTER EIGHT

Katrina sat wearily, watching her silent partner while he appeared to be deep in thought. Since the beginning of their partnership, he had never questioned any of her business decisions. He hadn't appeared to be interested in any of the decisions she had made, aside from occasionally patronizing their various clubs now and again. What could he possibly want now? She knew he had been to her latest endeavor, the Kat's Meow. To date, it was her pride and joy. There was something for everyone. Well, for those who could afford it, anyway. The women she employed there were impeccable. The overall atmosphere in all of her clubs was decidedly erotic, though not vulgar. She had worked hard to ensure that this club was the crème de la crème of adult clubs worldwide. If need be, she was wealthy enough to buy out her silent partner. She hoped it wouldn't come to that. He was vital in steering the clientele she was looking for to her establishments. His word alone was worth millions in membership fees among the very wealthy worldwide. She did to have to deal with criminals or other less desirables. She dealt with men who knew the game, knew how to keep their private entertainments private. It was a lucrative partnership on her end. She had no idea what he got out of it besides the thrill. He certainly didn't need the thirty percent profits, considering he had laid down all of the funds for the start of their secret little empire.

She squirmed in her seat a little as he rose to look out the wall-to-wall windows of his impeccably-appointed offices. Located on the corner of Decatur and North St. Peter Street, his top floor suite had an excellent view of the river. He stared at the waters, his hands clasped behind his back. At any other time, she might have enjoyed the way his suit jacket stretched across his broad shoulders, or the way his large, long-fingered hands rested against his pert, tight buns. He was seriously fine, for a white guy.

Unfortunately, she was much too preoccupied with why he had demanded she see him at eight o'clock on a Monday morning.

"Where did you find your night manager for the dancers?" her partner asked without turning to face her.

Katrina bristled. You didn't get as far as she had in the adult entertainment business without knowing your stuff. All of her employees underwent a detailed background check.

"He was referred by Maurice at the Baton Rouge club," she replied curtly. She didn't care for the soft-spoken question laced with malice. She didn't give a damn who he was, she would not be intimidated. "His background check was fine."

He turned to lift a folder off his desk and dropped it in front of her. She had to work to keep her hands from shaking as she opened it. The damn man was standing right behind her, demanding without words she read whatever it revealed. As soon as she began to read it, she felt like she'd been punched in the gut. Tim McIntosh was actually Tim McGuire, a two-time felon whose most recent arrest had been for aggravated rape. He hadn't been convicted because his accuser had suddenly packed up and moved out-of-state, refusing to return to testify against him. Because there was no DNA evidence, there was no case, and Tim went free. He changed his name legally, but that hadn't popped up on the background check.

Shit! This wasn't good. Her clients expected complete privacy. The last thing she needed was some low-life trying to blackmail her members. It would be the death nail of all her clubs, and could possibly spill over to affect her day job. As a corporate lawyer, many of her clients at the firm were also clients at her clubs.

"Thursday night he personally escorted me backstage for fifty bucks and encouraged one of your dancers to '*be nice to me*,'" he went on.

"Mr. Chevalier, those dancers welcome backstage visitors," Katrina assured him, though he was well aware of that fact. "I will take care of Tim . . ."

"*Most* of the dancers welcome backstage visitors." Thierry cut her off, his anger slowly burning through his calm façade. "But not Angelique."

Katrina swirled her head to stare at him in shock. Angelique had danced Thursday? She hadn't called to tell her that; she certainly would have made sure to be there when she did. It was just too damn dangerous otherwise. Remembering Angelique had also missed brunch on Sunday, Katrina felt a wave of fear wash over her.

"Angelique is fine," he told her, reading her emotions easily. "And Tim has already been taking care of."

Whatever that meant. She really couldn't care less. Her friends were the only family she had, as long as Angelique was safe . . . but then, how did he know that?

"How do you know she's fine?" she demanded.

Thierry considered not answering for a split second, but he knew Katrina would find out eventually. He had no intention of keeping their business relationship a secret from Angelique; he had no intention of keeping any secrets from her. She would accept him as he was or not at all. He was not ashamed of the fact that four years ago he had financed Katrina because she was her friend. Katrina had been subtly looking for a silent partner; he had made sure she had no need for any other than himself. It was a perverse way to get closer to Angelique, and it had turned out to work in his favor. He didn't begrudge a dime.

"She was with me," he answered, returning to his seat behind his desk. "She will be seeing a lot more of me."

Katrina couldn't have been more surprised if he had told her he was really the Pope.

"What do you mean, she was with you?" Fuck the partnership. If he had done anything to her girl, she was going to have to hurt him.

"I invited her to my house, and she accepted," he replied as if it was an everyday occurrence.

"Look, Angel isn't a working girl. She would never spend a night, much less a weekend, with some man she doesn't know. What the hell did you do to her?"

Katrina was standing now, fists posed on his desk like she was getting ready to leap over it. Thierry's lips twitched at the ferocious picture she presented. He supposed he would feel the same way had Piers, Remy, Aubrey, or Rance been threatened.

"I never once considered that she was anything other than the lady we both know her to be," he answered smoothly.

"Don't bullshit me!" Katrina hissed. "Angelique is not a toy to be played with and thrown away! You stay the hell away from her!"

"I am sorry, Ms. Smith, but I'm afraid staying away from her will not be an option," he replied calmly, "seeing as how I have every intention of making her my wife."

*****

Katrina had tried to reach Angelique for three hours without success. Completely frustrated, she had even called Solange, who she really couldn't stand, to see if she had heard from her. That had not gone well. Solange had simply stated that if she knew where her cousin was, she would definitely not be sharing that information. Katrina would have been amused if she wasn't so damned worried about Angel. Where the hell was she? Better yet, what the hell had possessed her to go to the club without at least one of them? On her last call, Katrina finally hit pay dirt.

"Yeah, I saw her this morning," Regina told her. "She said she forgot about brunch Sunday."

"And that made sense to you?" Katrina demanded. "That's just not like her."

Regina sighed. "Yeah, I know. Look, I really can't tell you where she was. Why don't you call her?"

"Like I haven't tried that?" Taking a chance, Katrina asked, "Did she tell you where she was Friday night?"

"Yes," Regina responded cautiously.

"Well, did you at least tell her it wasn't a bright idea to go there alone? Without protection?"

Regina was taking this doctor/patient confidentiality thing way too far. Angel wasn't her damn patient anyway! While Katrina respected more than most the way Regina would keep your secret under the threat of death, it could be damned irritating when you were trying to get information.

"Of course I did," answered an exasperated Regina. "But I understand why she did it."

"Of course you do," muttered Katrina. "Did she say where she was going when she left you?"

"No, but she received a phone call and left in kind of a hurry."

"Her mother, you think?" One thing that could force Angel to rush from one of her girls was her mother. Though they had all subtly tried to encourage her to cut the apron strings—Katrina especially—Angelique seemed to live in a constant state of fear of disappointing the cold woman.

"I don't know," Regina replied honestly, "but I don't think so. She seemed a little too happy for that. Anxious, but happy."

Regina had suspected it had been Thierry Chevalier, but she couldn't tell Katrina that without breaking Angel's confidence. Katrina, on the other hand, knew it was Thierry, and she had no qualms about speaking up.

"Did she tell you about Thierry Chevalier?"

"How did you know?" Regina gasped.

"I had a meeting with the man himself this morning," Katrina replied. "Let's meet somewhere quiet for lunch. Girl, you are not going to believe what I have to tell you."

It took less than twenty minutes for both women to meet in a small café in the Quarter. Because the area was always rife with tourists, locals tended to avoid places like these. Perfect for a little gossip. Though Regina still refused to give up all she knew, Katrina let her in on the formerly silent partnership as well as Thierry's declaration. They both agreed he had to know about Angel's current fiancé, though he seemed not to be too concerned about him. Of course, Regina could guess why after what Angel had told her, but she also knew Angel had not mentioned Paul's infidelity to Thierry. Either he had been investigating Paul Guidry, or he was extremely confident he could simply steal Angel away from him. Katrina insisted Thierry had investigated him.

"He investigates everyone," she assured Regina. "The man is meticulous. So, what do you think we should do?"

"Nothing," Regina replied. "Angel seems to be awakening into an independent woman we all knew she could be. We should let her."

"If it were anyone other than Thierry Chevalier, I would agree," Katrina groused. "But this man is way more than Angel can handle."

Regina shook her head. "I don't think so, but it's not our place to interfere in her life. We've been trying to encourage her to stop letting anyone do that."

"True, but I think the least we can do is keep a close eye on her," Katrina pushed.

"So, you think his little declaration was bull?"

"I don't know," Katrina admitted. "I just don't want to see her hurt."

*****

"You want me to do what?!"

Thierry lifted a sarcastic brow at Rance's uncharacteristic outburst. He would admit the request was unexpected to say the least, but Rance was never phased.

"I want you to draw up an incorporation paper for a new company," Thierry said again, slowly.

"Yeah, yeah, yeah." Rance waved his hand as he paced the floor. "But the part after that? The part about the sole owners you and who? Who did you say would have the final say in all decisions?"

"Angelique Dubois."

Rance gaped at his cousin as if he had grown a second head. To his knowledge, Thierry had never even met Angelique Dubois. From all that he had heard from the grapevine, she was a sweet kid, but rather empty-headed. She was nothing more than a figurehead for her mother's various charity endeavors. And Rance told Thierry so in no uncertain terms. He would have to be crazy to give her any kind of controlling interests.

"Look, if you want to make some kind of grand gesture to the community in general, start a charity and have her for some kind of spokesperson," Rance reasoned. "That would do Piers more good than having her running a damn company."

"You think I'm doing this for Piers?"

Rance had seen Thierry's infamous cold-eyed glare, when the blue turned icy and seemed to dominate the green. Never in the thirty-five years they had both been alive had that glare ever been focused in his direction— until now. Thierry voice had not risen, but rather gotten softer in that intimidating way he had. It was damned unnerving. Rance, a war veteran, found himself slightly afraid of his closest friend and cousin.

"Aren't you?"

"No."

He didn't expand on the single word reply, so Rance was forced to ask, "Then why? Do you even know Angelique Dubois?"

Thierry didn't answer, just smiled faintly and once again raised his brow. Rance considered himself to be something of an arrogant bastard, but he had nothing on Thierry.

"Look, Thierry, I don't know what you're up to, but I've never known you to throw away money."

"What makes you think that's what I'm doing?"

Rance couldn't answer that. He wanted to add that Lady Rienne was likely to have all kinds of fits when she found out, but he knew that would have the opposite of the desired affect. Thierry and Lady Rienne's personal feud was not known outside of the family. Thierry made an appearance at all family functions and most of the elder lady's charity or political functions, but he never darkened her door outside those events. To Rance's knowledge, they hadn't even had a conversation since Thierry was around twenty-six or so. There had been talk of an imminent engagement between Thierry and the granddaughter of Lady Rienne's closest friend in all the gossip columns from here to D.C. As soon as Thierry had learned of it, he had gone into their grandmother's private study for a talk. They were in there less than fifteen minutes. When they emerged, Lady Rienne was tight-lipped and pale, Thierry in an icy fury. He had left the house and had not spoken privately to her since that day. The fact that she might be infuriated by this unorthodox business move would mean less than nothing to him.

"I don't have any idea what you're doing, Thierry," Rance admitted. "I wish to hell I did."

Thierry smiled sadly, slapping his cousin on the back.

"You will," he assured him.

Just as Rance opened the door to return to his offices, Thierry called out, "Oh, and Rance?"

"Yeah?" Rance closed the door and turned back.

"Don't ever refer to Angelique as empty-headed in my presence again, okay?"

It hadn't been growled or yelled, but Rance felt the implicit threat down to his bones.

Angelique arrived at Thierry's office an hour after she received his call. She had to rush home to shower and dress, cursing her common sense every step of the way. She opted against driving. She didn't want anyone seeing her car and informing her mother. Thinking of her mother made her cringe. Charline had left ten messages, and Angel had yet to return her call. She just didn't feel like answering all the questions she knew were coming. No doubt Solange had informed her that she had been missing all weekend. Well, it wasn't anyone's business what she was doing or whom she was with. Though she loved Solange like a sister, the woman was an infernal snitch. She had learned to be extremely careful about letting Solange know too much.

Sitting in the reception area, Angelique looked at the clock once more. Okay, she had been here for twenty minutes already, and no Thierry. His secretary had directed her to the reception area, stating Mr. Chevalier was in a very important meeting, but had yet to inform him she was here. She knew because she had watched the woman's actions covertly since sitting down. Angelique realized the woman probably had no intention of informing him of her presence. Well, here was test one for Mr. Chevalier.

As if he'd been summoned, the office door opened, and Thierry escorted two men towards the elevators. She immediately recognized the shortest of the three to be Senator Thad Wagner of Texas. Her lips curled instinctively. The man was pushing for the public housing that had been unaffected by the hurricane to be torn down in favor of high-priced condos. He was also supporting more off-shore drilling and a refinery to be placed right at the mouth of the Mississippi. He saw Louisiana's tragedy as an excellent opportunity for Texas oil companies. Luckily, the men hadn't spotted her yet; she had a hard time keeping her immediate and instant dislike of the Senator under wraps. The man obviously had business with LeBlanc, Inc., which didn't bode well for the poor and the displaced. Strike one against Thierry. She made a mental note to pay closer attention when he talked about work.

He turned after the men had disappeared into the elevator, but still didn't notice her. He went straight up to the secretary.

"I am expecting Miss Angelique Dubois," he told the woman, looking distractedly at his watch. "Please send her in as soon as she gets here."

Just as he was about to stride into his office, the secretary looked up.

"Oh, she's here," she replied sweetly, pointing to the reception area.

Thierry barely spared the woman a cursory thank-you nod before turning on his heel to help Angel up.

"Hey, sugar," he whispered, kissing her hand, then her cheek. "Haven't been waiting long, I hope."

Angelique got the secretary's look of panic mixed with a healthy dose of fear. Good.

"Oh, I've been here for going on thirty minutes or so," she answered sweetly, her eyes still on the hapless secretary.

"Really?"

Angelique finally turned her attention to the man in front of her. "I thought you had forgotten about me."

Thierry hid a smile as he ushered her into his office and seated her on the couch off to the side.

"Make yourself comfortable, sweetheart. I'll be right back."

He left the door open as he excited. Angelique was quick to move closer to hear what he had to say to the witch who had left her waiting.

"Linda, is there any reason why you failed to inform me of Miss Dubois' arrival?" He asked the woman mildly.

The secretary sounded notably fretful as she rushed to answer him. 'You were in a meeting with the Senator, and she didn't have an appointment . . ."

"Have I ever consulted you on my personal calendar?" Thierry asked

"Well, no sir, but . . ."

"Part of your job is to inform me when people are here to see me. I expect for you to do just that. In the future, whenever Miss Dubois comes in, appointment or no, you will notify me without delay. Do I make myself clear?"

"Yes, Mr. Chevalier."

"Good."

Thierry strode back into the office, not stopping until he pulled Angelique into his arms to take possession of her lips in a kiss that made her forget her own name.

"Miss me, baby?"

God, yes. Had it only been five hours ago that he dropped her off at home? He had kissed her softly, telling her he'd seen her soon. To be honest, she hadn't expected it to be quite so soon, but she was glad he had called. She may be playing with fire, but he made her forget about Paul and her mother. She forgot how desperately unhappy she was with her life. When she was with him, it was easy to forget just about everything. With the help of Regina, Angelique realized she had lived her life for everyone but herself. Now, she had resolved to ride this out and see where it led. She would be careful, of course, but there was something about Thierry that she wasn't ready to give up. Hell, there was a whole lot about him she'd like to get to know a lot better.

"I asked Remy to go to the house and whip up something for lunch," Thierry told her. "Play hooky for the rest of the day with me?"

CHAPTER NINE

"Hey there, sweetness," Remy called as Angelique entered the kitchen, Thierry's arm firmly around her waist.

Thierry scowled at his cousin, but refrained from saying anything. It would only encourage him. Far from being tongued-tied today, Angelique and Remy bantered back and forth good-naturedly. Thierry might have been jealous but for the fact that her small, soft hand periodically caressed the arm wrapped around her whenever she felt him tense. He wondered if she even realized how in tune her body had become to his after one short weekend. His eyes crossed as he thought of the way she would be in bed. How long did it take for birth control to start working? He wasn't going to make it. Still, the prospect of her now svelte belly rounded with his child was not unwelcome. In fact, it was only making him harder. He just didn't want to trap her that way. He wanted her to tie her life to his

because she wanted to, not because she had to.

When he'd just about had enough of Remy

flirting shamelessly with his woman, he gentle nudged

Angelique towards the den, where they reclined on large

overstuffed pillows on the floor. Unable to keep his hands

to himself, Thierry played with the curls falling across her

chest, pulling one softly before releasing it to watch the

lock of hair curl back just as tight. He seemed so

mesmerized by the process, Angelique relaxed and let him

play. His other hand stroked over her body, sending tiny

little shivers all over. She had known this man for only

three days, and was already completely comfortable with

his touch.

"Let me ask you something," Thierry finally said.

Angelique turned her head and found herself

drowning in his turquoise gaze. A man this fine should

surely be illegal. If he asked her anything at all at this moment, she knew the answer would be yes.

"I asked you before if you loved your fiancé," he purred, his hand moving to cup her breast over her shirt while the other hand buried itself in her hair. "Now that I know the answer, I need to know when you're planning on calling off the engagement."

"And I would do that why?" Her voice was barely over a whisper. His touch was making it difficult to think.

"Because you are mine."

She barely had time to register the comment before his lips descended on hers. The hand in her hair tilted her head back, forcing her mouth open for his exploration. His tongue stroked, plunged, retreated, then stroked again. The hand that had caressed her breast softly and tenderly became more aggressive, squeezing and pinching until she moaned deep into his mouth, shifting with no effort at all until she lay directly beneath him. Her legs opened automatically, welcoming his hard bod

soft curves. He didn't hesitate to grind his very hard, very

large bulge into her very center, eliciting soft gasps. His

lips began to travel to her cheek, then to the very tender

spot just beneath her ear, causing her to arch her body into

his. She was unaware of his hand pushing her skirt up to

her waist, before disappearing beneath the waistband of her

panties, until she felt his long, thick finger stroking her

where she needed him most. She came apart at the first

stroke. She forgot all about her unwanted fiancé, the fact

that they were not alone in the house, and even the storm

she knew was coming with her mother. Nothing else

mattered but Thierry and the wonderful things he made her

feel.

"That's it Angel, baby," Thierry moaned in her

ear. "You're so beautiful. I love the way you come for me."

Thierry leaned back and made quick work of

disrobing her completely. Was there anything more

stunning than her milk-chocolate skin flushed and panting for him? Never had he met a woman so wonderfully responsive to his touch. It was as if she were created just for him. He had never wanted someone as much as he wanted his Angel right now. He had to taste her now, before she fully recovered from the last orgasm; he wanted her on that pinnacle again and again. Determined, he threw off his shirt before he buried his face between her thighs. His mouth literally watered as he inhaled her soft scent. Cupping her buttocks in his hand, he brought her up to his mouth, swiping her scrumptious little pussy before burying his tongue inside her. Nothing in the world could taste so good! He licked, sucked, and nibbled like it was his last meal, moving from her clit back to her now free-flowing pussy until she screamed, grabbing him by the hair, her body shaking.

He had wanted to wait. Lord knew he had only intended to make her come a couple more times before stopping. His hands seemed to have released his aching cock of their own accord. Even before he gave her one last lingering swipe of his tongue he was free, moving slowly up her body. The feel of his weeping member against the smoothness of her skin sent chills down his spine. Saints preserve him, he couldn't stop! Thank God he had enough of his functioning brain left to slide on a condom. He wanted to make her his permanently in the worst way, but he wouldn't do it by pregnancy.

"Tell me to stop, Angel baby, Angel, baby," he whispered even as he aligned his organ right at the mouth of her incredibly wet sex.

Stop? Was he crazy? She had imagined losing her virginity plenty of times, but never in a million years could she imagine this! Never had anyone made her feel so desirable, so sexy, so damn ready!

"Please," was the only word she could manage, even as she reached up to pull him towards her.

He didn't pause to ask again. With one powerful thrust, he plowed through the thin membrane separating him from paradise. It took every once of self-control he had, but he managed not to move, waiting until she adjusted to his size. She hadn't yelled, but she was squirming as if to find a more comfortable position. She was unbearably tight, and her inner muscles spasmed, holding him like a hot velvet vise.

"Please, baby, you have to stay still," he pleaded even as he began to move. "I am so sorry, Angel, baby, I have to move."

"Oh!"

The little declaration was music to his ears. He knew he was a bit larger than average. He'd worried he had hurt her, but looking down he saw the delightful wonder in her gaze, and he felt her legs move to clasp around his waist. Moving with excruciating slowness, he marveled at every expression that crossed her face. Her juices flowed freely while her pussy tightly clasped his cock in a stranglehold, and Lord, did it feel so good! Her every gasp and moan made him feel as though he were the most powerful man in the world. He watched her face carefully as he parried and thrust, noting what made her cry aloud, what made her catch her breath. It wasn't long before she was once again climbing the peak to completion.

Angelique had never felt so full. He stretched her to the point of pain, yet the small hurt couldn't begin to compare to the intense pleasure she never knew she was missing. Every single stroke not only caressed her clit in a glorious way, but was also hitting the much vaunted G-spot that until now, she had thought was myth. Within minutes she was shuddering with yet another orgasm, this one blowing all the rest he'd given her over the last three days out of the water. Stars exploded behind her eyelids; surely rockets were going off somewhere very near.

"Shit!"

Thierry had thought she had clenched him snugly before, but as soon as he pushed her over one more time, her pussy clutched him so hard he had to fight not to come himself. He watched in awe as her legs clamped on to him and her back arched completely off the pillow. Oh God, she was everything he had dreamed and so very much more. His testicles drew up insufferably tight, but he refused to let go of all these wondrous feelings. With a growl of pure satisfaction, he released the tenuous hold he had on his control. As he held onto her upraised hips, his movements became far more forceful, ruthlessly burrowing so deep she feared he might reach her very soul. She couldn't stop the frantic cries that fell from her lips.

"Please, oh God, Thierry, please!"

"Please what, baby?" Thierry demanded, his voice rough with insatiable need to brand this woman, to make her his, irrevocably. "Tell me what you need."

"Oh God, please don't stop."

He couldn't even if he'd wanted to. It wasn't until she climaxed a third time that he let go. With a groan that felt more like a whimper, Thierry shifted, carefully pulling his treasure on top of him without withdrawing from her cozy womb. He couldn't bear to separate himself from her, not yet.

"Is it always like that?" Angelique whispered into the sudden silence in the room so recently filled with cries of passion.

"Angel, baby, it's never like that," he replied, rubbing his hand up and down her spine.

"Then I was, I mean, it was okay for you?"

He gently lifted her upper body, careful to keep himself firmly seated. Cupping her head tenderly, he spoke firmly, keeping his eyes locked on hers.

"You were my wildest dream come to life. I swear to you, sugar, I will never want another woman. For me, there could never be another woman."

171

Angelique was trapped by the truth she saw in his eyes. He really meant what he was saying.

"What about your family?" *Or mine?* She left that part unsaid. His family was daunting enough without adding her dysfunctional clan to the loop.

"My family does not run my life," he stated flatly. "I won't give you up, sugar—not for my family, not for anyone."

*****

Angelique spent the next day contemplating her life at length, going over in her head all the things that had happened to her in the last few days. For the first time in her life, her self-reflections did not lead her into a great depression or cast a shadow of doubt on her future. She had no idea where this thing with Thierry was heading, but it wasn't about that. She needed to take some steps in her life to make herself happy, with or without Thierry. She had to start making her own decisions, living her own life. She wanted to be happy just being herself.

The first thing she had to do was break it off with Paul.

Angelique strode into the front doors of her father's office complex with pep in her stride and a smile on her face. Phase one of her new life meant giving Paul his ring back, along with a piece of her mind. While she probably would have married him if she hadn't met Thierry, this was not about her exciting new love life. This was about taking the reins of her destiny out of the hands of others. While Thierry might have awakened her to the possibilities, she was one who would have to make all the moves.

Not that he hadn't offered to deliver this message for her; after making love in the den, Thierry had made them a bubble bath in the massive Jacuzzi tub where they had made love again. After he had dried them both off and lay intertwined with her on the bed, he had brought up her odious fiancé.

"Sugar, if you don't want to face him, I would be happy to return his ring for you."

She had seriously thought about saying yes for a moment before shaking her head.

"No, it's something I need to do," she had stated firmly. This was her life they were talking about, after all. Besides, she didn't want to run from one controlling situation to the next. If she were going to exert some of her newfound independence, it was best to let Thierry know that right up front.

"Then I will deal with my mother," she went on.

"And then?" Thierry had asked softly.

"Then we'll see."

"Sugar, you've only known me for a short time, and despite what you might think, I am here for the long haul."

She hadn't known what to say to that. As much as she would have liked to stay wrapped up in his arms, she had to first stand on her own two feet. Luckily, he seemed to understand that.

"But I know you might not be ready for anything too heavy right now," he continued. "So I'm willing to wait, just as long as I can be a part of your life until you are ready to link our lives together."

If we haven't already, he mentally added. He had fallen so deeply for this woman, he knew there was no way in hell he would ever give her up without a fight. She was every bit as perfect as he had always known she would be.

Angelique was grinning openly by the time she reached the main elevators. She trusted Thierry in a way she had never trusted Paul. Some might call her a fool, but Thierry was never careless or reckless. She looked forward to exploring this new relationship and all it had to offer. They had made love one more time before falling asleep in each other's arms. She was delightfully sore today, but it was nothing she couldn't handle.

Smiling and greeting every one of her father's executives, she made her way through the large top-floor suite until she reached the top executive's receptionist.

"Miss Dubois!" the woman exclaimed. "Uh, let me call Mr. Guidry and let him know you're here."

Angelique had to smile at the woman's nervousness. So, the whole office knew of Paul's indiscretions. Perfect.

"Don't!" she said firmly.

The older woman looked taken aback at first, then a slow grin widened her face.

"As you wish," she said with glee, lowering her head to answer incoming calls.

Once again, Paul's secretary wasn't at her desk. *Oh, this is going to be perfect!* Angelique thought joyfully as she swept into Paul's office. Just as she had hoped, Paul had Tasha spread wide on his desk while he plowed away. She was so loud he hadn't even heard her entrance. She stood there and watched for a second. It seemed so tawdry to her now. Whereas before, she saw something she had never managed to inspire in anyone, now she saw the sordidness of it all. There was no love in this act. Listening to Tasha, she detected the woman was faking her overblown moans and cries. She wasn't sure how she knew, but she did. The only person getting off in this room was Paul. With a wicked smile, Angelique slammed the open door closed, causing Paul to jump back.

"Angelique!" he gasped, trying to pull up his pants and cover his very unimpressive genitals at the same time. "Honey, it's not what you think!"

She had to laugh at that one. "Really? Well, I think you're screwing your secretary. If it isn't that, what is it exactly?"

She waited while he sputtered some unintelligible

words, gesturing wildly in Tasha's direction. Tasha, being the smart girl Angelique had expected her to be, quietly dressed herself and slipped out of the office.

"Tasha, please wait for me by your desk," Angelique told her before she could make her escape.

The younger woman nodded and slipped out, closing the door quietly behind her.

"I swear this was the one and only time," Paul declared as soon as Tasha was gone. "And she—she seduced me!"

It looked like he was about to gather steam as his piss-poor excuse fermented in his head, so she decided to cut him off.

"The first time since last Friday, you mean." She put up her hand when it looked like he was going to dig himself deeper. "Look, forget it; it's not important."

The look of shocked relief on his face was downright comical.

"It isn't?"

There was so much hope in his voice, Angelique almost hated to burst his bubble—almost.

"No it isn't," she repeated. She was quite proud that she hadn't laughed in his face. But just as he smiled and began to make his way toward her with arms outstretched, his unfastened pants fell, tangling around his feet and causing him to fall flat on his face right in front of her. Angelique lost it. She might have been able to calm her loud guffaws had he not tripped and fallen again while trying to get to his feet. Bending down right by his face, she decided to put the man out of his misery.

"I only came by to give you back your ring and tell you the engagement is off."

When he opened his mouth to reply, she placed a single finger against his lips.

"This had nothing to do with Tasha, so please save your breath. Goodbye, Paul."

Standing once more, she placed the ring on his desk, then turned to the left, closing the door calmly behind her. Tasha waited at her desk, just as Angelique had asked. She was smart enough to start packing her belongings, but she hadn't run.

"Tell me what happened," Angelique told her quietly.

There was really no point in getting mad at Tasha. From what she had observed, Angelique was willing to bet the younger woman hadn't been all that eager to spread her legs for Paul. What she had mistaken for raw lust last week she now knew was all one-way.

"He told me he would fire me if I wasn't *'nice to him.'*"

Angelique nodded. She'd suspected as much. Quickly jotting down her cell number, she passed it to Tasha.

"Take a week off, then call me," she told her. "This time, I will be sure you have a safe job where no one will threaten you."

Walking out with her head held high, Angelique made a mental check on her list of things to do. *Step one down, one step to go*, she said to herself, smiling at the curious stares she received as she calmly strode back towards the main elevators, *then lunch with the girls*.

Angelique almost lost her nerve as she pulled into the long, winding drive of the beautiful whitewashed two-story mansion on St. Charles Avenue. Washing her hands of Paul was one thing, but dealing with her mother was something else altogether. This marriage was very important to Charline Dubois for some reason. The woman had immersed herself in wedding preparations, going over every minute detail with a fine-tooth comb. The engagement ball had been scheduled for August, a mere three months away. The arrangements had all been made, and down payments had been given. All that was left was

for the invitation designs to be selected, printed, and sent.

Thank God the actual wedding had been scheduled for next

May. Charline had not had time to finalize too many of

those details yet.

Standing outside the door of her mother's private

office, Angelique took a deep breath. *Walk in, make your*

statement, then leave, she chanted in her head, trying to

mentally prepare for the inevitable blow up. *Don't give her*

a chance to rattle you. Running her nervous hands down

the sides of her outfit, she took a few seconds to check

herself. She had chosen to wear a golden-bronze colored

silk shell to compliment her dark-brown lightweight

tailored skirt that stopped right above the knee. High-

heeled sandals and little teardrop earrings completed the

ensemble. She smiled to herself as she checked to make

sure none of her riotous curls had escaped the elaborate

twist on top of her head. Little ringlets framed the side of her face. Her hair was going to drive Charline crazy. The woman had forced her to straighten it since Angelique was a teenager. For some reason Charline went into a tizzy at the sight of her daughter's natural curls. Well, she'd be damned if she'd do it again.

Straightening her spine, Angelique swept into the room as if she owned it. She had to establish her independence from the outset or Charline would take the upper hand. *Not today,* she reaffirmed in her mind, *never again will I let anyone take over my life.* Charline had been studying samples of invitations spread out on the dainty antique desk. She looked up, ready to roast whoever dared to enter her domain without permission. Her jaw dropped at the sight of her daughter walking with a confidence Charline had never witnessed in her before. Her outfit was impeccable, her back straight, her eyes determined, and her hair . . . Charline narrowed her eyes, ready to lash out, only to be cut off before she could start.

"Good morning, Mother," Angelique said, sweeping into the room to stand right in front of the older woman as if daring her to say a word. "Going over the engagement ball invitations? Well, it's a good thing I caught you in time."

Who was this woman pretending to be her daughter? Angelique leaned down, examining the samples with casual interest before returning her gaze to her mother. Charline gasped. Angelique rarely looked at her so directly. What the hell was going on here?

"There is really no need," Angelique went on, as if she were discussing the weather. "After careful consideration, Paul and I decided to call off the engagement."

"What?" Charline sputtered, trying to wrap her mind around what she was hearing. Call off the engagement? And Paul agreed? That was impossible!

"We are no longer engaged," Angelique responded evenly. "A marriage between us would have been a terrible mistake. I will, of course, cancel all the arrangements you've made. I am sorry for all the time you wasted trying to make the party perfect for your only daughter, but I know you will agree it was best we found out how incompatible we are now rather than later."

She threw the last statement at her mother like challenge. What kind of mother would want to see her only child in a travesty of a marriage? Not giving Charline time to recover, she rounded the desk and gave her mother a peck on the cheek.

"I'll call you later, and we'll talk," Angelique assured her before turning and sweeping out of the room.

Angelique couldn't hold back a wide grin as she strode out of the house. She did it! Okay, she hadn't exactly given Charline a chance to reply, but it was best for now. Let her stew awhile. There was going to be hell to pay later, but she'd deal with it. *One step at a time*, she told herself

while driving away.

CHAPTER TEN

Angelique had waited until well into lunch at the popular restaurant she had chosen to meet Regina, Jade, Katrina, and Solange before she made her announcement. As she suspected, Regina, Jade, and Katrina were thrilled about her break-up with Paul. Though none of them had said a word, she strongly suspected none had ever liked Paul. Solange, on the other hand, had always championed Paul, and Angelique was burning to find out why.

"You did what?!" Solange exclaimed, looking at her cousin as if she'd lost her mind.

"I broke up with Paul," Angelique replied nonchalantly.

"Well, Hallelujah!" Jade exclaimed.

"I second that," Regina muttered, causing all eyes to turn her way.

"Well, you could have said something sooner," Angelique groused.

Everyone went to Regina for advice, including Angelique when she first became engaged. True, Regina hadn't seemed too happy with the news, but the only thing she'd said was to make sure this was really what she wanted.

"Angel, it was a decision you had to make all on your own." Regina shrugged. "I wasn't about to make it for you."

"Besides," Katrina interjected, "we all knew you would come to your senses sooner or later. You are a strong black woman; you just needed some time to realize it."

And maybe someone to put a metaphorical mirror right in front of her face, Angelique thought to herself.

"This calls for a celebration." Jade spoke up. "Tonight. Let's go to Bourbon Street and mess with tourists."

"Yeah," Katrina agreed. "Let's get torn up and call in sick tomorrow."

The conversation quickly turned into an animated discussion about places they could go and who would be the designated driver, while a quiet Solange stared at her cousin in shock. She had broken off the engagement with Paul? Shit! This wasn't good. Since when did Angelique start making decisions for herself? Where the hell was the reliable pushover she had always been?

"I'm sorry," Solange spoke up, breaking into the conversation, "but Angel, what the hell is going on with you?"

"What do you mean?" Angelique asked her cousin quietly.

There had been something niggling in the back of her mind about Solange. Her cousin had been almost as ecstatic about Angel's engagement as her mother. If any one of her friends knew of her initial doubts about Paul, it was Solange, but still for the most part she had pushed Angelique to accept the relationship as it was. Even when

Angelique had confided in Solange her initial suspicions

that Paul was cheating, Solange had tried to convince her it

was just nerves. Angelique had thought they were as close

as sisters, but she was beginning to rethink her relationship

with her cousin. It was true she hadn't run to her mother

about everything she did, especially stripping at Katrina's

club, but there were many instances where Solange had

gone to her aunt with various things Angelique had done or

was planning on doing. Like when she had applied to

graduate school in Boston. Or when she had applied for a

position with a New-York based company. That was one of

the reasons she had called everyone together for lunch. She

wanted to watch Solange's reaction to her little

announcement.

"I mean, Paul loves you! I mean, he asked you to

marry him. He wouldn't have given you up without a

fight," Solange told her, her face beginning to get red in

anger.

Interesting.

"A man who is really in love doesn't cheat," Angelique retorted.

"How do you know he was cheating?" Solange persisted. "You said it was just a feeling, right?"

"I caught him red-handed, Sollie," Angelique informed her. "With his secretary in his office. It was obvious the entire staff was aware of it."

Solange didn't just look shocked, she looked pissed. Angelique made a mental note of her cousin's body language. She wondered if Sollie was even aware of all the information she was inadvertently giving her.

"How do you know the whore didn't seduce him?" Solange demanded. "Think about what you're doing, Angelique! How can you be so damn selfish!"

Angelique leaned back in her chair. "How is breaking off *my* engagement to a cheating snake being selfish, Sollie?"

There was absolute silence at the formerly boisterous table. All eyes were focused on Solange, who saw nothing more than her cousin.

"You are not the only one affected by this marriage, Angel!" Solange hissed, in full fury. "What am I supposed to do now?"

"What does my marrying or not marrying Paul have to do you with you?" Angelique asked pointedly.

She had been right. Solange was knee-deep into something with Charline, something that hinged on her marrying Paul. But what? Angelique was determined to find out.

"Good afternoon, ladies."

A collective gasp was heard around the table as Angelique let that now familiar deep, sexy voice wash over her.

Thierry had to smile at the shocked expressions turned his way as he slid in next to the chair where

Angelique was seated. Behind him, Piers, Aubrey, and Rance were equally as stunned as he leaned down to place a soft kiss on his woman's lips. Remy, damn his soul, was grinning like a Cheshire cat.

"Hello, sweetheart," he murmured against Angelique's lips.

She hadn't shied from the very public declaration of intimacy, which was a good sign. He was making headway. He'd been unsure of her reaction—not that he had any idea he would see her here. He was taking his cousins to lunch to inform them of his impending departure from LaBlanc and the reasoning behind it. He hadn't wanted to blindside any of them, especially Piers if he decided to run for Congress. He wasn't naïve enough to think his relationship with Angelique wouldn't affect them all in some way. He had been a member of society for far too long to be disillusioned in any way about people's view on interracial relationship, especially in their social and political circle. As much as he would like to believe the country in general had progressed, he knew people would do a lot more than talk. Business partners would disappear into the woodwork, invitations would cease, and whispers would become a dull roar. They would never accept Angelique in any inner circle. He hoped to minimize the damage as much as possible, which was part of the reason he was getting out now.

Having the chance to be with the woman of his dreams was really just an excuse for quitting. Had he wanted to, he could easily have remained at the helm of the family's many businesses and business interests, daring anyone to say anything. He wasn't above using every method in his considerable arsenal to ensure the woman he intended to make his wife was happy. He was tired of his life as it was. There was no satisfaction in making money hand over fist. There was no thrill in keeping the family empire intact and prosperous. He was sick of the phony friends, shady businessmen, and grasping women. It was all so—plastic. Very little was genuine or real in the world of old political power and even older money. There was very little purpose outside of the acquisition of power. What he found with Angelique was real, it was tangible. Every moment they spent together was more precious to him than anything else in this world. He wasn't about to let that feeling go.

Finally looking up at the rest of the women at the table, he acknowledged the only other person he knew. "How are you, Katrina?"

Katrina looked towards Angelique, visibly relieved at her friend's little nod and smile. Thierry had told her about their business relationship.

"Thierry," Katrina acknowledged.

"These are my friends: Jade, Katrina's law partner; Regina; and my cousin Solange," Angelique pointed out.

"Ladies," Thierry nodded at each of them as Angelique introduced them. "The tongue-tied cowards standing behind me are my cousins Piers, Aubrey, Rance, and Remy."

There were mumbled hellos and general awkwardness. Thierry and Angelique were obviously oblivious to anything but each other.

"Well, it was nice meeting you all," Thierry stated after a minute, sparing a glance at the women openly goggling the interplay in front of them. Leaning down, he whispered in Angelique's ear. "I'll see you later tonight, sugar," he promised.

Solange stared in horror as they kissed again before Thierry moved away with his cousins in tow. Oh God, Angelique was seeing Thierry Chevalier? This was much worse than just breaking up with Paul.

"What the hell is going on here, Angel?" Solange demanded.

It took Angelique a moment to refocus on her cousin. Frowning, she considered the other woman. Yep, something was definitely rotten in state of Denmark.

"Again, I have to ask what the hell my personal life has to do with you, Sollie?"

Angelique didn't raise her voice; she didn't need to. All eyes at the table now turned to her in shock. Angel was the soft-spoken one, the one who always sought to resolve conflicts within the group. This new assertive woman was a shock. A delightful shock, but a shock nonetheless.

Solange turned deep red. She was exposing too much, she knew.

"I—I just care about you," Solange stuttered. "Angel what are you thinking? Thierry Chevalier is way out of your league! He'll chew you up and spit you out. Please, tell me you're not sleeping with him!"

It was Angelique's turn to blush. She turned her flushed face away from her cousin.

"Holy shit! You lost your cherry!" Katrina whispered in gleeful awe. "Spill it girl, how was it?"

"Oh, my God! You said you were seeing him; you didn't say you were sleeping with him!" Regina put in.

"Wait, Regina knew you were seeing him?" Jade asked. "When the hell did all this happen?"

As Angelique was busy trying to answer all the questions from the three women she personally never could stand, Solange quietly slipped from the table and out of the restaurant. She had to go see her mother and Aunt Charline to inform them of the recent developments. Something was going to have to be done, and soon, or they were all screwed.

Angelique noticed Solange's sudden departure but said nothing. No doubt she was on her way to see Charline. All Angelique had to do was find out why.

"Well?" Jade was saying. "How did all this happen?"

Angelique gave her the same abbreviated version she had given Regina privately earlier. She knew Katrina knew a little more than what she'd confessed to Regina. Thierry had told her all about his previous dealings with her friend. She had grilled him as to why he would be Katrina's silent partner, providing all the initial capital, based on the sole premise Katrina was her friend. She wanted to know what he had expected from such a deal. What she had learned about Thierry over the short time she had known him was, he never did anything without motive. Feeling as though she knew Thierry far better than he let most people, Angel understood that in his way, Thierry had done it to feel closer to her. It seemed he had often been there, hovering in the background of her life, though she never known of his presence. It would creep some women out, and was dangerously close to stalker-like; but for some unfathomable reason, Angelique understood.

Thierry tended to hide his emotions under a layer of steel. He never allowed anyone to questions his actions. He had let her probe every aspect of his life, leaving out nothing. She was humbled by his trust, and the least she could do was trust him a little in return.

"You have to admit, if you were going to date a white man, you can't get much better than him," Regina sighed.

"Are you saying you wouldn't date a white man?" Katrina demanded.

"I know I would if it were one of the Chevalier boys," Regina sighed. "That is one seriously fine family."

Jade shifted in her seat, pushing her half-eaten food around her plate.

"I don't think I could," she said after a minute. "I mean, I don't think I could get over all the history, you know? And who needs the dirty looks and snide remarks?"

"Girl, free your mind and your ass will follow," Katrina snorted. "I would date any guy who treated me the way I deserve to be treated. Black, white, or whatever."

"Hey, Jade, didn't you have a case with the lawyer?" Regina asked. "What's his name again?"

"His name is Rance," Jade answered, thankful for her dark-chocolate complexion that hid the sudden rush of blood to her face. "And I didn't have a case *with* him. I represented a former worker suing LeBlanc Shipping."

"Whatever." Regina waved her hand. "Why the hell didn't you mention he was so seriously sexy?"

"I didn't notice," Jade lied.

"I never knew you felt that way. About interracial dating, I mean," Angelique said, going back to Jade's former comment.

"Look, I'm not against it," Regina assured her. "It's just not for me."

"Famous last words," Jade assured her. "With the serious lack of eligible men in the city now, I don't give a damn if the man were green as long as he was gainfully employed."

"Don't forget straight," Katrina added.

"And single," Jade laughed.

"And knows how to work with what he's working with," Angelique said, causing the other women to stop and stare at her before they all dissolved in a fit of giggles.

*****

"What was that little scene all about, Thierry?" Rance demanded as soon as they were seated far from the table of women they had just run into.

Thierry lifted an eyebrow at the other man. Rance may have been a year older than he was, but he had never answered to him or anyone else. He had every intention of telling him so, but Remy beat him to the punch.

"Who the hell pissed in your beer?" Remy asked his brother, scowling.

Rance ignored his twin, determined to get answers.

"First the company bullshit, and now you're kissing her in public?" Rance went on. "What he hell is going on between you and Angelique Dubois?"

"One would think that was obvious," Thierry replied dryly.

Recognition hit Remy like a freight train. No wonder she looked so familiar. Oh, this was getting good!

"Are you fucking insane?" Rance asked incredulously. "What game are you playing, Thierry?"

Thierry had expected this reaction from Rance. His entire life had been tied up in being a Chevalier. Like his father before him, Rance had attended West Point and stayed in the military until recently, when he came home to become the head of Chevalier and Associates, the family law firm, after the death of Aubrey's father. His own father, General Boden Chevalier, was currently a leading official at the Pentagon. Rance had been the one grandchild who never gave Lady Rienne a moment's worry, always making the right steps, being seen with the right women, associating with the right people. Thierry wasn't really sure if he did so out of a sense of obligation, or if Rance really bought into the bullshit.

"What's with you, Rance?" Aubrey asked quietly. "You act like he's done something to you personally."

That was unexpected, but Thierry would take support where he could. He didn't give a damn what other people thought or what they would say, but he had to admit Rance's vehement reaction hurt. The four of them were closer than brothers, sharing the horrors of having grown up under Lady Rienne's controlling eagle eye and high expectations. He'd never thought any of them to be bigots or racists. Now that he looked at Rance, he wasn't so sure.

Rance exhaled harshly, running his hands through his hair. He was actually starting to sweat. He knew he was sounding like a racist ass, which couldn't be further from the truth. He couldn't tell Thierry why he was acting the way he was, not now anyway. He had planned on it, one day, but now that plan was all blown to hell. Thinking hard, he tried to come up with a plausible excuse.

"I'm just worried what it might do to Piers' campaign," Rance offered lamely. "You know how vicious primaries can get ,and the party could see an opportunity to steal a seat in Congress here."

"Who said I was running?" Piers asked.

"Are you?" Thierry asked, turned his gaze full force on an uncomfortable Piers.

"I'm still thinking about it." It was a cop out, but at this point it was all Piers was willing to offer.

"I wanted you all to know about Angel," Thierry told them. "That's part of the reason I asked you to lunch."

"Part of the reason?" Rance went on. "What next? Are you going to marry her?"

"Absolutely," Thierry said simply, causing each other man to regard him in complete shock. "But what I really wanted to tell you was I am giving each of you my stock in LeBlanc, Inc. I will divide it equally between all of you, which means Uncle Boden will have controlling interest. I will be leaving the company altogether in a couple of weeks."

He sat back to let them absorb that little tidbit. The only who didn't seem the least bit surprised was Remy, who sat drinking his beer, looking as though he had personally orchestrated this move. At least one of his cousins was sincerely happy for him. That this would infuriate Lady Rienne was an added benefit to Remy's mind, no doubt.

"Is she worth it?" Aubrey spoke up first, surprising them all.

"Hell yeah," Thierry answered without a second's hesitation.

"Then I'm happy for you." Aubrey said quietly. "Good women are hard to come by."

That made them all wince. They had all forgotten Aubrey and his disappearing wife. After his night out, he seemed to have dismissed it completely.

"Aubrey, you don't have to go through with the divorce, you know," Rance told him. "I can still stop it."

Aubrey shook his head.

"It's not that I want her back," he assured them. "It's just that I never should have married her in the first place. I let someone else choose my spouse for me, never questioning whether it was the right thing to do. I couldn't even say I liked her. I barely knew her at all. Hell, I don't even remember what she looked like."

"About five-foot-six, five-foot-seven, blonde hair, hazel eyes and really big teeth," Remy supplied without missing a beat.

"You know there is something seriously wrong with you, right?" Thierry told him.

"Hey, I'm on your side," Remy exclaimed, throwing up his hands. "Angel is one hell of a catch. Sweet as pure cane, pure as the driven snow—at least she was."

"Remy, shut up now and I won't kill you," Thierry warned.

"Remy knew about this?" Rance demanded. "You told him, but you didn't bother to let the rest of us know?"

Thierry shrugged, unwilling to answer the question. Maybe it was because Remy, like himself, had cut all ties with Lady Rienne. On some level he knew Remy would never give the vicious old woman the chance to interfere.

"Maybe because he knew I had no desire to prance around the countryside in a sheet and hood," Remy challenged Rance.

"I am not a racist!" Rance insisted.

"Then what the hell is your problem?" Remy threw back.

Rance didn't answer. He couldn't. Instead, he watched his hopes go right down the toilet. Thierry was the only one who could stop any machinations Lady Rienne could think up. Now he would be too busy stopping her from trying to ruin his life to help Rance with his little dilemma.

"Look, I just want you to be sure," he told Thierry. "I support you in whatever you decide. And there is nothing wrong with Angelique Dubois as far as I know. I'll bring those papers you asked for to your office this afternoon. By the way, who is going to take your place at LaBlanc?"

"Your father," Thierry told him.

Rance nodded, then stood to leave, afraid of revealing too much if he stayed.

"Wait up, Rance. I need a ride." Aubrey said, getting up also. "I'm happy for you, Thierry. Don't ever let her go."

Aubrey studied Rance as he navigated the downtown traffic. He knew all his cousins thought him absent-minded. Well, he was somewhat, but he was also observant. Because they often dismissed his presence, the guards each of them had learned to erect at an early age were often let down around him. He knew far more about each man than they thought—Rance particularly. He knew what was eating away at him.

"Why didn't you tell him?" Aubrey asked after a while.

"Tell who what?"

"Tell Thierry the real reason you were upset."

Rance looked over at Aubrey. He couldn't know, could he?

"What are you talking about, Aubrey?"

"Jade Jessups."

Rance slammed on the breaks in the middle of the street, causing cars to swerve around him.

"Who . . . where did you hear about Jade Jessups?" he asked slowly, his ears ringing. He had never told anyone; he hadn't even wanted to examine it too closely himself. He thought he had time to plan carefully before making his move.

"You did," Aubrey informed him. Seeing Rance's confusion, he explained. "You remember that case you lost? I think it was about a disgruntled employee from the shipyard or something like that. It's not often you lose a case. You came over to listen to yourself talk afterwards. Every other sentence was about Jade Jessups. What she wore to court, the way she smiled at her witnesses, how she intimidated your witnesses when she was cross-examining. You seemed more perplexed by her than by the fact you lost the case."

Well he'd be damned. He usually went over to talk to Aubrey, but he never thought the other man was actually listening. He always seemed too engrossed in whatever musty book or document had caught his attention at the time. Aubrey always seemed far more interested in the past than anything happening in the present.

"Fuck," Rance muttered, moving with the flow of traffic once more. "You scare me, Aubrey. I suppose you know far more about all of us than we ever realized."

"Except for Thierry," Aubrey admitted. "One never knows what he's thinking or what he'll do next. I have never seen a man in such complete control of his own world."

Amen to that, Rance thought to himself. He just hoped Thierry had carefully planned this latest move.

Rance had a feeling this just might change more than

Thierry's own life.

CHAPTER ELEVEN

The last person Angelique expected to greet her at the front door when she got home was Paul. He sat on the front porch looking like he'd just lost his best friend, a bouquet of red roses in his hands. Too bad she hated roses.

"Please leave," she told him as she walked past to unlock the door.

"Angelique, please, just give me a chance to explain," Paul pleaded. "Then if you still want me to leave, I'll go."

Angelique looked back at him. There was no reason why she should.

"You have five minutes," she told him, holding the door open.

It was a mistake, she knew it was, but she wanted to be the one with a clear conscience. Let him have his say, then kick him out. He was probably only here to save his job anyway. She watched wearily as he took a seat on her couch, then patted the area beside him. Yeah, right.

"I'll stand, thank you," she informed him, leaning against the wall with her arms crossed.

"Angelique, I'm so sorry," he said morosely. "It was just . . . well, I was so wound up, and I wanted to wait until the wedding with you. I know I don't deserve a second chance, but sweetheart, I swear, it will never happen again."

Until the next time, Angelique thought to herself.

"Paul, if you are here to try to save your job, you can save your breath. I have no intention of telling my father the real reason we broke up."

"Is that what you think this is about?"

Oh God, he actually managed to look hurt. Why couldn't he just take the bone she threw him and go on about his business?

"I *know* it's what this pathetic apology is about."

215

For a split second, she could have sworn she saw fury burning in his gaze, before he quickly banked it.

"Angelique, I love you," Paul insisted, getting up and moving towards her. "We can be so good together."

"Stop right there," she warned, shoving against his chest before he could embrace her.

Okay, now she was pissed. She knew she had let him and her mother walk all over her, but at no time did she ever give him reason to think she was stupid. Gullible, maybe, but never stupid.

"I don't know why you think I'm an idiot." Her voice was controlled, barely. "Let me assure you, I'm not. This was never about love, and you damn well know it. You wanted into the business; well, you got it. Take it and leave me the hell alone."

All pretense of the loving, remorseful lover was gone in a flash. Paul narrowed his eyes as he reached out to grab her by the arm.

"You think this about my damn job?" he

demanded.

"Isn't it?" Angelique lifted her chin, refusing to

be intimidated.

"There is a lot a stake here, little girl," he hissed,

moving his face close to hers. "Whether you want to or not,

you will marry me."

"Paul, I wouldn't spit on you if you were on fire,"

she retorted.

Paul tightened his grip on her arm. It hurt like

hell, but there was no way she was going to show any

weakness. Her right hand moved to the lamp by her side. If

the asshole got physical, she was going to brain him. She

might bash his head for general principle if he didn't let go

of her damn arm.

"You don't have to love me," Paul jeered in her

face. "You don't even have to like me, but you will marry

me. For your sake, for you mother's sake, for your ditzy-ass cousin's sake, you will be Mrs. Paul Guidry."

Angelique narrowed her eyes. Oh, no, the hell he didn't! Without thinking, she let her knee fly straight to his unprotected groin.

"You bitch!" Paul screamed as he immediately released her and dropped to the floor, gasping. "Oh, I am going to make you pay for that!"

Reaching the end of her patience, Angelique stepped forward to stomp down on the hand covering his crotch, then kicked him in the head for good measure. How dare the asshole think he could come in her house and threaten her. She was seriously considering kicking him again . . . when a strong arm clutched her waist.

"Hold on, baby girl. You want him well enough to leave, don't you?"

Thierry. Her body relaxed against his at the first touch. Thank God she hadn't locked the door behind her.

She had genuinely been tempted to do some damage to the jerk rolling around on her floor in agony.

"Did he hurt you?' Thierry asked while nuzzling the side her neck, his arms still wrapped around her protectively.

"No," she assured him. "But I think I might have hurt him, just a little."

Thierry didn't bother holding back the laugh that bubbled up at her confession. He always knew she was a little tigress; she just needed someone to let her out of her self-imposed cage. He kissed her cheek.

"That's my girl," he murmured in her ear, sending delicious chills down her spine.

Paul slowly rose to his feet and gawked at the two people standing in front of him. Angelique and Thierry Chevalier. When the hell had that happened? Seems he should have kept a closer eye on his little fiancée. It was much worse than her breaking off the engagement or finding her backbone. She was involved with the most powerful man in the state. Paul felt the first stirring of real doubt. If she didn't marry him, he was going to be ruined. No matter what she might think, there was no way in hell her father was going to let him stay at the helm of the family's business unless he was officially a part of that family. He hadn't wanted to give Paul the job in the first place, thinking to give him a honorary title with no real power or authority. It had taken Charline weeks to talk her husband into giving him the position Paul currently held.

"Angelique, tell me you're not seeing this man," Paul tried, playing the concerned, repentant boyfriend.

"I don't see how our relationship has anything to do with you," Angelique responded imperiously.

Thierry hid his smile in her hair. Paul looked like he had been sucker punched. Good. After what he had found out about Paul recently, he wanted the other man to know exactly who he was dealing with.

"Sweetheart, he's playing with you." Paul sounded desperate, but damn it, he was. He could only hope that was really the case. "He's probably seeing you to ruin your father so his cousin won't have any real competition running for Congress. He's not serious about you, honey. I am."

Paul fervently hoped he was right. He could put one over on Adam Dubois, but only because the man though he was in love with his daughter. He couldn't hope to put one over on the shrewdest businessman known to man.

Angelique tilted her head to the side as she witnessed Paul thinking of everything he could to place doubts about Thierry in her mind. She had, of course, thought of that possibility at the beginning. But the more she got to know Thierry, the more unlikely that seemed. Thierry was ruthless when it came to something he wanted, or something that meant a lot to him, but he wouldn't use an innocent woman to destroy his enemy. Besides, when she was with him, the way he looked at her, the way he touched her, was very real. Some women lived their entire lives without ever having a man look at them the way Thierry looked at her. Like she was the sexiest and most precious woman in the world. Paul had definitely never looked at her like that.

"Are you done?" Thierry asked.

Paul's attention snapped from the woman he had believed his own to the man stranding behind her. Thierry was casually stroking her arms in a manner that was far more intimate than he'd ever been with her. Sudden understanding dawned on him.

"You slept with him, didn't you?" Paul demanded. "You dirty little slut! No decent black man would want you now! It wasn't enough for you to shake your ass in front of a bunch of rich white men! No, you had to go spread your legs for them too!"

One moment Paul was raging at his ex-fiancée, the next he was pinned to the wall, his feet dangling off the ground, and Thierry's hand wrapped around his throat.

"Don't ever talk to her like that again," Thierry warned softly. "Or I swear by God your mother won't have a body to bury."

Paul's eyes bulged out of his head as he faced what he was sure was death in the face. He nodded as much as he could, praying the other man would just let him go. Thierry sneered. God, he hated weak men who threatened women. There was nothing more pathetic. Sure he had gotten his point across, Thierry dragged Paul to the door, then literally threw him out.

Paul landed on his face in the front yard. Luckily, there was no one around to witness it. Gritting his teeth, he stormed to the car, his mind feverishly working up another plan. If he lost his job, which was sure to happen now, he was finished. He couldn't let that happen. Not only was he looking at total financial ruin, but he would probably wind up in jail. He should have fucked Angel and gotten her pregnant. How the hell was he going to fight Thierry Chevalier? He had to go talk to Charline. She had as much at stake here as he did. She had damn well better find a way to control her daughter. Once he managed to get her to say "I do," there was going to be hell to pay. He would make her pay dearly for his humiliation, if it was the last thing he did.

"Are you all right?" Thierry asked, pulling Angelique into his arms.

"I'm fine," she stated. "More than fine, actually. To think I almost married that man."

She shivered at he thought. Would she really have gone through with it? She'd like to think she wouldn't, but she wasn't so sure. Why had it taken Thierry to show her how sad her life had been? She had spent so much time trying to make everyone but herself happy, and look where that had almost taken her. And what the hell had Paul

meant, saying her mother and her cousin would be sorry?

She had to find out what was going on between the three of

them.

"Hey." Thierry broke into her musings. "Where'd

you go?"

"I was just thinking about some of the things Paul

was saying."

Thierry lifted her chin to force her to look at him.

"Think about that later," he told her.

"Yeah? What should I be thinking about now?"

"This," he murmured, his lips descending to hers.

There was nothing soft about the kiss. It invaded

her very soul, seeking complete surrender, which she gave

gladly. When her arms moved to wrap around his neck,

Thierry lifted her, moving against the wall. He pressed

against her, his hips grinding against hers. She wrapped her

legs around his waist, glorying in the feel of his hot

225

erection against her core. His hands moved to cup her buttocks, pulling her even closer.

"That's it, Angel, baby," he encouraged. "Show me what you need."

Angelique whimpered as she pushed herself closer, rubbing her clit against the hard bulge in his jeans. Thierry could feel how wet she was through his pants. Groaning, he tried to tamp down the growing need to be buried deep inside her. She was bound to be sore; he had only intended to kiss, touch, and maybe caress a little today. He wasn't going to make it. Damn, he had never felt so completely out of control as he did with his Angel.

"Please, Thierry," Angelique whimpered, grinding hard against him. "I want to feel you."

With a growl, he ripped her panties right off her body. Somehow, he managed to free his rampant cock from his pants with one hand and in less than a minute was sinking into her.

"God, baby, you're so tight," he groaned, resting his head against her shoulder while restraining the impulse to drive into her like a wild man.

"Am I doing it wrong?"

His head snapped up at the question. Her beautiful brown eyes stared wide-eyed at him with such innocence that he almost came right then.

"Not doing it right? Angel, baby, if it was any more right I think I might have a heart attack."

He could no longer hold off moving, watching as he slid in and out of her divine pussy. *My pussy*, he mentally amended. His own slice of heaven on earth. God, he had to get her naked and beneath him, but Lord knew he couldn't stop. With every whimper that escaped her lips, he grew more aggressive, stroking harder. She was delectably responsive, holding nothing back from him. Whimpers turned to cries of ecstasy urging him on faster, harder. He could feel her tightening on him as she moved with him.

"That's it, sugar. Give it to me. Come for me."

Angelique's legs constricted around his waist as she climaxed so hard she saw stars. Still he didn't stop, not letting her come off her high. As soon as one orgasm ended, another began. She felt as though she were made of nothing but nerve endings. There was nothing she could do but feel.

"Oh God, baby, I can't hold on."

Who asked him to? She held onto his neck for dear life as he rammed into her for all he was worth. It should have hurt, but Lord, it felt so good. When he exploded inside her, she went with him, loving the feel of him giving her everything he had.

"Where is your bedroom?" Thierry rasped, still buried deep inside her.

"Upstairs to the left."

He carried her up as they were, anxious t[c]

to the bed to strip her completely. As soon as he ste_ .

through the door, Thierry hardened inside her.

"Shit!" he exclaimed, taking in the décor.

The pillows and sheets were pure white. Just

imagining them against her dark skin made him want to

come again. The coverlet was white with tiny pink flowers

all over it. The massive canopy bed was also white, as was

every other piece of furniture in the room. There was a

rocking chair in the corner by the window holding a giant

teddy bear. There was another, smaller teddy bear on the

bed. The virginal bedroom brought every dirty little fantasy

he'd ever had as a horny teenage boy rushing back. Oh, the

things he would do to her in this room.

"It's childish, I know," she murmured against his

chest.

"It's perfect."

Swiping the teddy bear out of his way, he laid her in the middle of the bed and stripped as fast as his hands would go. She watched him languidly, making his already hard dick even harder. She had no idea how decadent she looked, sprawled on the bed with her skirt bunched up at her waist, her nipples visible through the little shirt.

"Undress for me, sugar."

Unable to help himself, he reached down to stroke his cock, watching as she rose to her knees and drew the shirt over her head. The white lace bra she wore underneath left nothing to the imagination, but he wanted to see her in nothing but her skin. Her hands moved behind her, unzipping the skirt, then lying down to shimmy out of it. Jesus, the sight of her waxed little pussy made him want to cry at the beauty of it.

"All of it, Angel, baby. Take off the bra."

She took her sweet ass time until finally the perky mounds his mouth watered for were completely bare. Her chocolate-colored nipples seemed to be taunting him. He had to taste them.

Angelique let out a little yelp as Thierry literally dove for her, capturing her wrist to bring her hand over her head.

"Hold on to the headboard and don't let go," Thierry ordered.

Angelique swallowed harshly. He appeared feral as he looked over her nude body. His lips covered her right nipple while his hand pinched down on her left.

"Oh!" she exclaimed, reveling in the strangely delightful contrast of pleasure and pain. When he switched sides to repeat the action, she almost came.

"Thierry, please!"

"Please what?"

His lips traveled up her chest to her neck, where he bit down, then sucked where he'd bitten. She bucked involuntarily, her body desperately seeking what it needed.

"Tell me, Angel, baby. What do you want?"

"You," she whispered brokenly, eliciting a chuckle from him.

"I'm right here, sugar."

His hands traveled down her torso to her needy pussy, but they didn't enter. She yelled, bucking once more when he pinched her clit, then flicked it. Oh God, what was he doing to her?

"Thierry!" she screamed.

"Yes, sugar?"

"I need you inside me, please!"

Thierry shifted his body to cover her completely, careful not to enter her no matter how badly he wanted to.

"Look at me, Angel."

When her eyes flew to his, he cradled her face in his hand.

"Tell me exactly what you need inside of you," he demanded.

"Your, um, penis."

Thierry smiled ruefully. Close, but not quite.

"Say *cock*," he told her. "Tell me you want my *cock* deep inside your *pussy*."

Angelique shivered at the way he said it. She had never used the words in her life, but he made them sound so . . . *delicious*.

"Thierry, please give me your *cock*. Put it deep inside my *pussy*."

Thierry nearly howled at the sound of it. Grabbing her hips, he entered her slowly, loving the way she tried to raise her hips to force him deeper.

"Nope," he told her. "You are a very bad girl. I'm going to have to punish you."

Holding her hips still, he went as slow as possible for as long as he could. But the way her back arched, the way she pleaded so prettily, he was soon plunging as deeply as he could go. When her legs wrapped around his hips, he lost it.

"Damn, Angel, baby, it's so good!"

She wanted to agree with him, but she couldn't speak. Higher and higher he drove her until she was seeing stars. She screamed out his name, her back leaving the bed while her legs crushed him closer.

"Fuck!" Thierry yelled, following her over the ledge as her pussy clamped down, milking all he had.

It took a few minutes for him to come down enough to shift to her side, pulling her closer to him so that her head lay on his chest. He knew it was probably too soon, but he had to say it.

"I love you, Angel, baby."

"You barely know me."

"Oh, I know you all right," he assured her.

"Oh, yeah? And what do you know, precisely?" she challenged.

"I know you're my Angel."

CHAPTER TWELVE

Charline was in a cold fury. First, the ungrateful little brat had decided she suddenly wanted to make decisions for herself; next, the slime of a man dared to threaten to cut off her funds if she didn't get "her child" in line; and now, an old dragon was sitting in front of her demanding that she keep the brat from the old woman's precious grandson. As her head began to throb in earnest, Charline battled to keep the red haze of rage from overwhelming her. She couldn't kill the old woman; too many people would miss the old bat. Damn Angelique to hell and back! She had been nothing but trouble from the moment she was conceived.

Not only had she broken the engagement Charline had worked very hard to arrange for her, but now the little whore was sleeping with the most prominent bachelor in the state. From what Paul had said, her new lover was fiercely protective of her. That was not a good sign. Surely he would tire of her soon, after the novelty of screwing the black mayor's daughter had worn off. The problem was, they didn't have time to wait. However oblivious Adam was to his only child, he loved her. As soon as he heard Angelique had given Paul his walking papers, he would either fire or demote him. Thanks to Paul's stunning lack of common sense, his immediate termination was far more likely than a simple demotion. Just like a man to screw up what should have been a simple problem. He should have come here immediately, but no, he had to try to fix this mess all on his own.

Arienne Chevalier knew when she was being ignored, and the mayor's wife was most definitely ignoring her. It grated her nerves to be driven to this course of action, but there was no hope for it. Thierry, much like his grandfather before him, was hell bent on destroying all that she had endeavored to achieve. Unfortunately, she had nothing to blackmail Thierry with, and also like his grandfather before him, the damnable man had planned

ahead. He had controlling interest in LeBlanc, Inc., he had

personal fortunes stashed around the world, and he owned

more minor companies than she knew about. From the time

he left her home to go to college, he had either been

planning for a complete break with the family, or a

complete takeover. The problem was she wasn't sure

which. She couldn't depend on the remaining three of her

four beloved grandsons. They knew about Thierry and this

girl, and not a one had brought that information to her.

They had always been close; they did grow up together

after all. She would have thought that something as serious

as this would have surely challenged their bond.

Apparently not. Not even Piers, who had the most to lose,

had said a word. In fact, they were all avoiding her.

Another ominous sign.

Unfortunately, she was very sure how serious

Thierry was about this little slip of a woman he was seeing

now. Somehow, the mayor's daughter had managed to find a way past the layers of ice Thierry encased himself in. For the past three weeks he had been seen escorting the woman around, dancing attendance to her every need. The grapevine had it either he slept at her home or they both spent the night at that home he had recently bought—again without her knowledge—in Faubourgs Marigny, of all places. Her sources were impeccable, but they never seemed to manage to inform her of Thierry's moves before he made them or even immediately following. Unlike the others, Thierry alone was impossible to spy on or figure out. She did know his habits though. He left work early for this woman, cut meetings short whenever she arrived at his office, and spent weekends disappearing to that house of his. Not only that, but he took her on shopping expeditions and to the movies, of all places! This was not typical Thierry behavior, which meant this was far more serious than a fling. Thierry had fallen hard. Hopefully she could but an end to this before it was too late. If only she could get this flighty, selfish bitch's attention!

"Mrs. Dubois," Arienne spoke into the growing silence in the room, gaining the other woman's attention at long last. "I came here out of respect to your husband's position in the community. Something must be done, and it must be done quickly. Sometimes young people cannot see the forest for the trees. But we both know this relationship cannot continue. I am sure that in your community, much like my own, this kind of thing is frowned upon."

Years of planning and scheming had placed Charline in the position she currently enjoyed. Adam had not been an easy catch. The things she had to do to get him to marry her . . . Well, that was neither here nor there. But she would be damned if she'd let some shriveled uppity witch play the queen in *her* house!

"What things, Mrs. Chevalier?" Charline implored sweetly. She knew what the woman was implying. Let the crone spell it out.

"Well, Thierry and Angelique dating, of course," Arienne replied in the same overly nice tone. "And please, call me Lady Rienne."

Charline grit her teeth to keep from tearing the old woman's hair out by the roots. *Lady* Rienne indeed. As if Charline herself wasn't every bit the lady the old woman claimed to be!

"Oh, I am sure they are just *good* friends." Charline decided to pretend ignorance. Let *Lady Rienne* think what she would. Thierry Chevalier was not her problem. "Angelique is a good girl. She recently has been having . . . difficulty with her fiancé. I am sure your grandson is only trying to help. They are business partners, after all."

Charline could tell by Arienne's expression she hadn't known that little tidbit. She didn't bother to hide a smirk at her superior knowledge.

"Yes, well, *appearances* are everything!" Arienne recovered after a heartbeat. Business partners? Oh, this was much worse than this silly bitch knew. "Why, I have even heard rumors they've been seen sleeping together! Can you imagine?"

"In public?" Charline feigned shock. "I assure my daughter would do no such thing!"

"Not in public," Arienne ground out. "They have been seen entering each other's residences and not emerging until morning."

"But my dear Mrs. Chevalier, one would have to stand outside their homes the entire night to ascertain that!" Charline laughed. "The very idea is preposterous!"

"Yes, well, these things have a way making the rounds. It can't be good for your family's image. I mean.

Boys will be boys. But for girls, my dear, there is never an excuse." Arienne smiled with malice.

"Yes, but I fear what ugly rumors might do for your other grandson's political aspirations!" Charline added before the other woman had time to glory in her direct hit.

"Or you husband's," Arienne couldn't help but add.

Stalemate. Both women stared at each other, giving grudging respect. Still, Charline could smell desperation on Arienne she couldn't cover up. There was nothing she could do to stop Thierry from seeing Angelique. If he were half as ruthless as he was rumored to be, he had probably but his grandmother in her place long ago. Charline almost envied Angelique for having found a real man. Too bad she couldn't allow it to last. Thierry could not be manipulated; therefore, he was of absolutely no use to Charline.

"I'll talk to Angelique," Charline said, finally rising. "I am sure there is nothing to worry about."

Taking her cue, Arienne also rose to be escorted out of the mayor's home.

"I could not ask for more," Arienne lied. "Such a shame this younger generation is lacking in propriety. They think nothing of their families and what they suffer as they go chasing an impossible dream."

"Yes, interracial dating seems to affect the families far more than it does the couple involved." Charline couldn't resist twisting the knife a little.

Arienne stiffened, but otherwise did not acknowledge the comment. What could she say? She knew it was far more damaging to the Chevaliers than it was the Duboises. Still, the Dubois clan was a very old Creole family. They would want to keep the bloodlines every bit as pure as she wanted to keep the Chevalier's. She had failed once; she very much feared she would fail again.

******

Angelique entered her parents' home with a healthy dose of trepidation. She knew this day was coming, though she had managed to put it off for three weeks. It had been a mistake to put it off. As before, she didn't bother knocking at her mother's office door. She simply walked in, her head held high, and sat in a chair in front of the desk.

"I have been calling you," Charline started in an even, temperate voice. Angelique was well aware of the storm brewing just beneath the surface.

Strange, but she wasn't afraid of her mother's rages anymore. In the past, the mere thought of upsetting Charline would have terrified her.

"Well," Charline went on. "What do you have to say for yourself?"

"I'm sorry for not calling you?"

Okay, so maybe glib wasn't the wisest course of action, Angelique thought as she watched her mother turn various shades of red. Being pure blood Creole, Charline could never hide when she was either mad or embarrassed. Her cream complexion gave away most of her emotions.

"Paul is beside himself," Charline said, choosing to overlook Angelique's comments. She could usually guilt the girl when she became a little too willful. This situation was outside the norm, but she was still her mother. If Angelique could be counted on for one thing, it would be trying to please her mother. Charline had used that against her many times, and it had never failed.

"That's too bad for Paul," Angelique replied.

"Really, Angelique! This had gone too far. You have made your statement, now it's time to break off whatever you think you're doing with the Chevalier boy and get back together with Paul."

"I wasn't aware I was making any statements," Angelique stated.

Charline was not amused. "You will break up with that Chevalier boy!"

"Thierry Chevalier is no boy," she informed her mother. "I assure you he is all man." *My man,* Angelique mentally added.

"And what do you think will come of this?" Charline demanded. "He won't marry you. Old money marries old money; they do *not* marry black women, regardless of background."

"Well, I am from old money, so I have one out of two going for me." Angelique's reply dripped with sarcasm. It may not be shrewd to antagonize her mother, but it was fun.

"You know as well as I do you are hardly right for those people!" Charline informed her. "And you are far from a shade that could possibly make it more . . . palatable!"

Here was the bane of her entire existence laid bare on the table. She had never been the right shade for Charline Dubois. She was horrified to have produced a dark-skinned daughter. She had let Angelique know what a disappointment she was in so many different ways. And Angelique had allowed her mother to hurt her on innumerous occasions because she was ashamed of not being what her mother had wanted her to be. Honestly, it still hurt to know her own mother found her lacking over something that she had no one control of; no one did.

Lifting her chin and refusing to show how much her mother's comment hurt, she replied evenly. "Like I said before, Thierry is a grown man. His family does not control his actions any more than I will allow you to control mine."

There! She had laid down the gauntlet. Charline's face went from red, to a pasty white, and then to a deep red infused with purple. The older woman stood and walked around to lean right in Angelique's face.

"You. Will. Obey. You will marry Paul. Period. This so-called *relationship* with that *man* will end now!"

The sneered words were barely whispers, said with a malevolence intended to intimidate. Angelique was quaking inside, but she refused to show it. Damn it, she had let her mother run her life for the last time! It didn't matter whether or not Thierry planned on marrying her. Wherever their relationship went, she wanted to enjoy the ride. Mentally squashing her inner fears, Angelique held her mother's gaze and stood her ground.

"There is nothing you can do to make me marry that philandering bastard." Her words were said every bit as quietly as her mother's had been. And as she said them, she felt her courage build. "If and when I decide to stop seeing Thierry, it will be because I *choose* to, not because you or anyone else ordered me to."

She really should have expected the slap that nearly knocked her off the antique Victorian chair. The loud CRACK echoed throughout the room. Holding the delicate arms of the chair, Angelique stared at her mother in disbelief. Why the hell was marrying Paul so important to her? It made no sense. She could see her mother being upset about the preparations and unavoidable excuses to nosey friends and acquaintances, but there was no reason for the ferocity of her anger.

"Listen, you ungrateful little brat! You will marry Paul. You will not ruin this for me. I didn't raise you out of the kindness of my heart to have you turn on me!" Charline ranted.

"I will not marry Paul." Angelique was surprised by her even tone. "And generally, it is a mother's duty to raise or help raise her child."

"I am not your damn mother!" Charline screamed. "You are nothing but the bastard of a slut! I agreed to raise you as my own, feed you, clothe you, try to make you into a lady, but obviously blood will tell! You are as much of a whore as the bitch who whelped you!"

Angelique sat in stunned silence as Charline's venom ripped her to her very soul. Charline was not her mother. She had never loved her, never even wanted her. All the times she had struggled for any crumb of affection from the woman she'd believed to be her mother had been hopelessly futile. All the years she had wasted trying to be the person Charline had wanted her to be were years spent chasing an impossible dream. She looked at the stranger before her with new eyes. Charline was a bitter woman, haunted by some perceived wrong done to her in years past, and Angelique had always been the outlet for her frustration.

But what did that say about her father? This man had given his child over to a woman who obviously hated her. Was his political career so important to him that he sacrificed his only child, his own flesh and blood? Angelique did not believe for one second he loved Charline; he could barely stand to be in the same room with the woman. He was never home. Her father had only been on hand at special events, birthdays, and holidays, and even them he tended to lock himself in his study for the most part, never bothering to observe how his child might be faring under his wife's care.

Standing in a daze, Angelique turned to leave, only to be stopped by a harsh grip on her arm.

"You are not leaving here until you agree to marry Paul," Charline hissed. "It is the least you can do! It is your duty to your name, to me!"

Angelique shook her head at the woman's delusions. Any sense of duty she might have felt, this woman had killed. Yanking her arm away, she started walking towards the door.

"Damn it, Angelique! Come back here! You owe me this! You owe it to your name! Your heritage!"

"I owe you nothing," Angelique told her firmly without bothering to turn around. "And as far as my name,

I will decide what does and does not honor my family name. I am a Dubois born and bred, no matter who my mother is or was. You just married one."

*****

Angelique drove straight to her father's offices at city hall. Once past security, she strode straight to his office, ignoring his secretary who tried to stop her, and went right in.

"Angel!" Adam exclaimed, looking up from the massive city map he had been studying with three of his closest aides. "What's wrong, sweetheart?"

"I need to talk to you now," she told him, careful to keep her composure when all she wanted to do was scream at the top of her lungs.

"Honey, we are in a very important meeting right now . . ." Adam began, but his daughter would not be put off as she had so many times in the past.

"This can't wait, and I seriously doubt you want an audience."

Adam was taken aback. His Angel was a biddable girl, never making waves, never causing problems. The fact that she was here meant there was a problem. Mentally castigating himself, he excused his aides and steered his daughter to the small couch off to the side of his spacious office.

"What is it, sweetheart?" he asked worriedly. "Is it Paul?"

Angelique felt the tears she had managed to keep in starting to fall, first as a trickle, quickly becoming a small stream down her face.

"I broke up with Paul over three weeks ago," she told him brokenly.

"Why didn't you tell me?" Adam questioned. "What did he do?"

"I never wanted to marry him in the first place," she told him. "It wasn't as if your wife gave me much of a choice."

"What does you mother have to do with any of this?" Adam was confused. Why hadn't Angelique told him about the breakup? For that matter, why hadn't Charline mentioned anything? Last night she had talked as if everything was proceeding as planned. She had even requested he clear his calendar for the engagement ball and other festivities. "Why didn't you or your mother mention this to me?"

"I have no idea why your wife failed to tell you," Angelique couldn't keep bitterness out of her voice. "As to my mother, how would I know what she tells you? I don't even know who she is."

Adam should have known this day would come. He should have prepared himself for the questions that would come with it. The truth was he had hoped and prayed

Angelique would never find out about the colossal mistakes he had made in the past. Mistakes that had cost the only woman he would ever love her life. His daughter was coming to him for answers, but what could he say?

"Oh, Angel," he sighed heavily. "I am so sorry."

What more could he say? He should have told her, but there had never been a right time or the appropriate situation. To be honest, he had hoped Charline would be the one to talk to her. She was a woman, and women were good at breaking things gently.

"You're sorry?" Angelique was incredulous. "For what? That I found out, or that you left me in the care of a heartless bitch who showed me nothing but disdain all my life?"

Adam was shaken by his daughter's statement. Charline and Angel had always been close.

"Honey, you don't mean that." Adam took her into his arms. How long had it been since he had given his daughter a hug? He had been working too hard. But with the hurricane and all the other pressures of being mayor, he never had the time. "You're just upset," he soothed. "You and your mother, Charline, will make up."

Angelique shook her father off and sprang to her feet.

"I don't know whether you are deliberately blind, or maybe you never wanted me either," she ground out. "Close? Charline and I were never close! I am too dark, too undignified, my hair is too nappy, I don't know how to dress! Hell, your wife thinks I can't manage to decide which man is right for me! And you think we're close? The woman just accused me of being a whore—just like my mother! She informed me I was *lucky* she deigned to raise me! Maybe you would have recognized something was wrong had you even been around!"

Dear God, what had he done? All this time he had been grateful Charline had agreed to bring up Angelique as her own. In fact, it had been her idea. He had never even considered marrying Charline until he found himself in need of a mother for his newborn daughter. He had taken for granted that Charline wouldn't resent raising his lovechild.

"I didn't know," he whispered brokenly.

"Who was she?" Angelique demanded.

Adam slumped against the couch. She deserved to know no matter how badly the memories hurt. Even after all this time, he felt like he was that thirty-year-old fool he had been back then. He had fallen in love with Naomi Jefferson hard. From the first moment he saw the saucy student from Algiers, he had wanted her. He had been a junior professor at St. Xavier, just about to run for city council. She had been a student. She hadn't teased him or come on to him; he'd deliberately set out to seduce her. Being the handsome arrogant son of a former mayor, he had thought to sleep with her a while, then move on. But he had fallen for her instead. His father, the elder Mayor

Dubois, had found out about their clandestine affair and

had hit the roof. No son of his was going to carry on with

some poor dark-skinned girl. It didn't fit his perfect image.

His mother had tried to help. She had said his father was

"color struck," believing light-skinned Creoles were

genetically superior. Unbeknownst to Adam, his father had

threatened Naomi and her family. He owned the home they

rented, he employed her father. He told Naomi's parents to

take the girl out of state, away from his son. No one knew

Naomi was pregnant at the time.

The family had relocated to the Mississippi Gulf

Coast. No one could have predicted Hurricane Elena would

tear the small house they had settled into apart. Adam had

found his Naomi barely clinging to life, her belly swollen

with his child. Doctors couldn't save her, but they had

managed to save the child. Only after Adam, Jr. threatened

to leave the country with all he had left of Naomi did

Adam, Sr. relent and allow him to bring his child home. Sometimes Adam wondered whether or not his father had known about the pregnancy, and if so, would he still have done what he had? Probably.

Charline had been from a decent Creole family. They were not rich or prominent, but they were pure Creole and Adam, Sr. had approved. He never would have considered marrying her if she hadn't agreed to raise Angelique as her own. She had suggested they live abroad for a few years, then return with the toddler, no one the wiser. It had worked. Despite Angelique's darker complexion, no one had questioned her parentage. His political career was able to pick up right where it left off. He realized now he had made a deal with the devil. In order to achieve his own personal goals, he had failed his child. He could see it in her eyes as she listened to his story: the contempt, the anger. She walked out as soon as he was done, without saying a word. He very much feared he had lost his only child.

Why was Charline so hell bent on this marriage that she would blow up like this? She had as much to lose as he did by letting the truth be known after all this time. She enjoyed her position as the mayor's wife. She liked being a famous Dubois even more. Paul's family was not powerful; the Guidry family was not one the leading families in the community, nor did they have much money. Adam had put his wife on a budget years ago, after she'd showed she couldn't manage money to save her life. It would make sense if she were getting some kind of monetary compensation from all this. In fact, if he hadn't given Paul a job, for Angelique's sake, the young man wouldn't have very much to offer his daughter.

Suddenly, Adam remembered a message he had shrugged off before: Thierry Chevalier had called regarding something about Paul. He had put it off because he thought it was probably about this upcoming bid for Congress.

Everyone was expecting one of the powerful businessman's

cousins would run against him. Maybe he had some

information about Paul. He hurried to return the phone call,

wondering what in the world Thierry Chevalier had to do

with his daughter.

CHAPTER THIRTEEN

Thierry sat back in the booth of the seedy bar,

contemplating whether he was brave enough to take a swig

of the cloudy glass mug of beer before him. Judging by the

sticky floor and the equally sticky table, the chances that

the glass was even half clean weren't good.

"I wouldn't drink that."

Thierry raised his brow at the man who placed a

unopened bottle in front of him as he slid into the opposite

seat, opening his own bottle, then handed his key chain

bottle opener to Thierry.

"And you picked this place why?" Thierry asked,

grateful for the bottled beer.

"Off the beaten track," the man offered.

"What did you find out?" Thierry asked.

Didier DeCapêt was Thierry's information man. He

had no idea how the man found out all the things he did, he

just knew that Didier could be trusted with the most

sensitive assignments. Part of it might have been the way the man looked. With lightly tanned skin, cool gray eyes, and midnight black curls, he could pass for a number of different nationalities and had the uncanny ability to blend in. It was strange that a man standing well over six feet with a powerfully formidable build could go about unnoticed, but Didier did. Possibly the air of danger that surrounded him made people look away quickly, not wanting to invite his attention, so they failed to notice anything distinguishable about him. His uncle Boden had referred him to Thierry, and Boden Chevalier didn't trust lightly. He had worked faithfully for Thierry for going on ten years now.

"Your Grandmother visited the mayor's wife. The meeting didn't go well, if her agitation was any indication. She has been trying to contact all your cousins, but they have all been unavailable. Not long after she left the mayor's house, your girl's cousin and aunt showed up, stayed for about an hour and a half, then left looking a great deal more assured than they came."

So Thierry was right about Charline, Solange and Anne—Solange's mother—Dubois. They were all working with Paul. Now he just had to make sure Paul was doing what he thought he was.

"I want you to check out my suspicions about lover boy," Thierry told him. "And if he goes to see the mother or the cousin again, get pictures."

"Did that," Didier said, sliding a sealed manila envelope across the sticky table.

Thierry grimaced as he picked it up, causing Didier to laugh out loud.

"When do you want to meet again?" Didier asked.

"I might be going out of town for a week or so," Thierry told him. "Call me as soon as you get something."

"And your grandmother?" Didier asked.

"Keep an eye on her and let me know if she contacts anyone I should be concerned about."

*****

Angelique drove around for over an hour before she found herself at Thierry's office. She really hadn't intended on running to him, yet here she was. Laying her head on the steering wheel, she let out a heavy sigh. One month. She had been seeing the man for one month and here she was, ready to share her family's dirty little secrets. She hadn't even considered going to Katrina, Jade or Regina; not with something this serious. Somewhere along the way, she had come to trust Thierry implicitly. She should just drive away and drown her sorrows in a serious chocolate binge. She was probably ten kinds of a fool. After all, she'd never even suspected Charline wasn't her real mother. She should have. She looked nothing like Charline. The older woman was an only child, but she had never even met Charline's parents when they were alive. Now she understood why her grandmother had left her all of her money and controlling interest in the family businesses and stipulated in the will none of the funds or stocks could be in any way administered by Charline. Angelique had thought all this time her grandmother had simply wanted her to assert her independence.

A sudden knock on her car window jarred Angelique out of her glum musing. Thierry. Great. So much for driving away.

He didn't wait for her to roll down the window. He opened the door, pulling her out and into his sinfully strong arms. One deep breath of that clean, masculine scent unique to him, and the dam broke. God, it just felt good to be held for no other reason than that he was happy to see her. He had no clue her world had just been shattered by the heartless selfishness of her parents. How long had it been since she was embraced by someone who wanted nothing more than what she would willing give?

"What's wrong, sugar?" Thierry had seen many women cry before. Some cried seeking to manipulate with tears, some cried because they couldn't comprehend not having their way, some even cried about losing the lucrative position of being his latest arm candy. There might have been a rare occasion where the tears had been real. Generally, Thierry had been very careful to only date women who knew better than to expect anything more than what was on the surface.

Faced with the tears of the woman he loved more than life itself, Thierry felt a pain unlike any he'd ever felt before. Hell, he didn't even know what was wrong, and it hurt like a ragged dagger straight to the heart. Lifting her by the chin, he couldn't help but notice the slight discoloration against the dark skin of her left cheek. The skin was slightly red and inflamed. It probably wasn't noticeable to most, but he had spent their every waking second together memorizing everything about her. He knew that when her brow creased slightly, she was trying to work something out; when she bit her bottom lip, she was concentrating; when she bit her upper lip, she was trying to fight her arousal. Right now she was hurting, and he had never felt so helpless in his life.

"Angel, baby, who slapped you?" He kept his voice light and even. He didn't want to scare her, but he very much wanted to tear someone apart with his bare hands. *Please let it be Paul, God, please.* That the man had dared to manhandle her once before was a good enough reason to kill him, but he had promised Angel to let it go. He'd be damned if he'd let it go this time. Careful to keep his body relaxed, he pulled her in tighter against him. "Tell me who hurt you, sugar."

"My mo—Charline," Angelique mumbled against his chest.

He couldn't stop himself from tensing. Didier didn't tell him Angel had been back to her parent's house. But then again, Didier had been with him. There wasn't a heck of a lot he could do to her mother. Still, he made a mental note to have a few words with her.

"No! You will not go talk to her!"

Thierry looked down to find Angel glaring at him through her tears. He smiled in spite of himself; she could read him better than Piers or Remy at this point. She probably didn't even realize how good they were together. He couldn't resist bending down to kiss her tears away. It infuriated him to think of anyone hurting a woman so naturally sweet and loving. Of course he would talk to Charline Dubois. He had to make it very clear to the lady that whatever she did to her daughter, she did to him, and Thierry Chevalier did not take kindly to being fucked with.

"I mean it, Thierry!" Angelique warned. She didn't want another confrontation with the witch. She didn't want anything more to do with the woman she had previously thought was her mother. A clean break was what she needed.

"Of course you do, Angel." He kissed her again to close the subject. "Now are you going to tell me what's wrong?"

"Not here." How pitiful would it be to just cry it all out right here in the parking lot? Out of the corner of her eye, she could see people coming and going, all very interested in seeing who Thierry was holding, and in public no less! Not like he had ever tried to keep their involvement a secret. He took her to restaurants where they were sure to be seen. He walked boldly down the street with his arm securely around her shoulder. He blithely ignored the pointed looks and practically dared comments. So far, no one had said a word to either of their faces, though she knew rumors must be swirling around town like wildfire.

Funny, a month ago she would have been terrified of all the talk they must be inspiring. Now she couldn't care less. What had this man done to her?

"Okay." Thierry broke into her thoughts, pulling her away from her vehicle. "Come on, we'll take my car."

Angelique pulled back a little. "We can take separate cars," she said, looking down at her sensible little compact.

"I'll have security drop your car off at the house," he informed her, bending to sweep her up in his arms. "We'll take my car."

She didn't want to fight the issue. Given all that she'd been through today, it wasn't really worth fighting over. She did make him put her down before he approached the security office on the ground floor of the building. They were on their way out when they ran into his secretary, Linda, returning from what appeared to be a very late lunch.

"Mr. Chevalier!" Linda exclaimed. "Were you looking for me?"

Thierry raised his brow at the woman's preening. What on earth made the silly woman think he was looking for her? He watched shrewdly when she finally spotted Angel, her face showing contempt before she managed to get herself under control. Interesting.

"Oh, well," Linda went on when he didn't answer her. "Senator Wagner has been calling. He said to tell you he was in town and anxious to get in touch with you."

"Thank you, Linda. I will be out the rest of the day." Dismissing her, he grabbed Angelique's hand and started walking towards the door.

Linda watched his departure with a mixture of frustration and anger. For five years she had worked for that man, and not once had he even noticed her. If there was one thing she knew for certain, it was that she was an extremely attractive woman. She could have her pick of any of the other executives that worked here. But the arrogant ass that was Thierry Chevalier had never seen her as anything other than a damn secretary. And now to prance around with the mayor's daughter? It was disgusting!

Making her way up to the door and into Thierry's private suite, Linda didn't hesitate to open his office door to rifle through his desk. Lady Rienne had offered her a very generous amount of money to find out anything she could about her grandson and his disgusting affair with Angelique Dubois. Well, that was exactly what she was going to do! Grinning evilly, Linda came across just what she was looking for, a receipt for what appeared to a luxury escape for two to Paris, France leaving tomorrow morning.

"Gotcha," Linda whispered, making her way back to her desk to call Lady Rienne. If anyone could put a stop to this disgusting affair, it was the old dragon lady. Maybe then Linda would have a chance.

Thierry lay wide awake, staring at the ceiling.

Angel had finally drifted off to sleep draped across his

chest. After pouring out the entire odious tale of Adam and

Charline, he was more convinced than ever that whatever

Paul was up to, Charline Dubois was neck deep in it with

him, as was Solange and her mother. There was no doubt in

his mind Paul was blackmailing Charline, but why ask for

Angel instead of money? Not that Angel wasn't a prize.

God knows he didn't think he could survive if anything

were to happen to her. She was the very air he breathed.

But Paul certainly didn't want or need her the way that he

did. There was only one answer: Dubois Enterprises. Paul

was not only broke, he and his family were swimming in

massive debts. Adam Dubois might be blind, but he was no

one's fool. Thierry had discovered Adam hadn't given Paul

his current position until months after the engagement was

announced.

That explained Charline and Paul, but not Solange or her mother, Anne. Didier was still working on possible connections between Paul and the other two women, but whatever it was, it was buried deep. Now that Angelique knew Charline's secret, they were bound to get more desperate. He had been planning on taking Angel away for a while, but maybe it should be sooner rather than later.

The feel of soft, warm lips sprinkling butterfly kisses across his chest brought Thierry's mind back to the woman who lay beside him. In all the times they had made love, Angelique had never initiated it, at least not physically. She certainly knew how to make him hard as a rock using nothing more than a look of invitation. And the lip biting thing—that was enough to drive him crazy. He felt his body relaxing at her exploratory kisses and cute little nips. No matter how badly he wanted to feel her pinned beneath him, writhing as he drove into her like a wild man, he wouldn't. He could not, however, stifle the groan that escaped his lips as she slowly moved lower.

He held his breath when he felt her shift, moving between his legs. She was hesitant, moving down a little and stopping to kiss or lick the skin of his lower torso. He almost came out of his skin when her little tongue swiped at his inverted belly button. He could feel his cock slowly weeping for her, like it was begging to be placed where it belonged. When her kisses moved to his upper pelvis, he clenched his jaw. Damn, the woman could make him feel like a teenage virgin just by her touch.

"Touch me, sugar." He could have kicked himself as soon as he said it, but he couldn't help himself. He knew he'd be all over her at the first touch of her hand.

Instead of the hand he was expecting, Thierry felt soft lips, followed by a warm, wet tongue on his achingly taut cock. She stayed there for a moment, swirling his

very tip. He was gasping now. God, he

anything so sweet.

Holy shit!" he yelled when her mouth sank down,

and he knew he was going to die right then.

His hands gripped her by the hair, intending to push

her away. There was no way in hell he could last like this.

But he found himself moving her head, helping her find a

rhythm as he slid in and out of her hungry little mouth. His

heart was beating so hard he could feel it banging against

his chest. Each time she descended, she managed to take a

little more, suckling ravenously on each upstroke. He had

never even thought to ask her to do this previously; he

knew he would have a hard time holding back. In the back

of his mind he worried about pushing her too far, but the

suction she was creating, the way her tongue slid down his

flesh, the way she relaxed completely when he pushed a

little more—he was making his way down her throat before

he realized what he was doing. She had by no means taken

all of him, but she was coming damn close. When he gripped her hair a little harder, pushed a little deeper, the needy little moan that she emitted was his undoing.

Looking down, his heart stopped. Watching his Angel swallow him was an erotic rush far more potent than any of his fantasies. She was watching him, taking in every expression, her eyes burning with passion that equaled his own. It was so beautiful he could feel the prickling of tears stinging his eyes. He felt his testicles tighten in the tell-tale sign he was about to come—hard.

"Angel, baby, I'm going to come." He tried to move back from those scrumptious lips, but she followed him, moaning around his dick. The vibrations were too much. Thierry exploded like a rocket.

Angelique didn't move. He half-expected her to scurry away as he erupted into her mouth, but Lord love her, she swallowed every drop, her tongue giving him one last swipe before sitting up.

"Was that alright?" she asked tentatively, biting her upper lip.

She was underneath him before she could blink. Though they hadn't made love earlier, Angelique had her clothes off automatically when she climbed into the bed, and he had followed suit. He hadn't wanted to do more than hold her, comfort her. She'd had a hell of a day. Thierry silently sent a prayer of thanks there were no clothes between them now. He didn't think he'd have the patience to take them off. Angel seemed to understand his frenetic need to be inside her. Her legs opened to welcome him as soon as her back hit the mattress. He slid into her, gathering her body close, loving how wet she was for him. Every time he sank inside her, he felt like he was coming home.

"I love you, baby," he whispered, kissing her everywhere he could reach. "God, sugar, I love you so much."

Angelique felt tears prick behind her eyelids. It felt so good, so right. Thierry completed her in a way she knew no one else could. He not only filled her body, but he filled her heart and soul.

"I love you, too," she whispered.

Thierry came to a complete stop. Pushing himself up on his arms, he looked down into her eyes.

"Say it again," he rasped, holding perfectly still.

"I love you."

He plunged, then retreated slowly. "Again."

"I love you, Thierry. Please make love to me! I need to feel you!"

He lost it. Coming to his knees, he held her hips to thrust over and over again, watching the way she arched and thrashed against him. Her dark skin was erotically stark against the white sheet. Not even the sunrise was as beautiful. Even as he poured into her, he didn't stop. He couldn't even if he wanted to. He took her higher and

higher, even as sweat rolled off their skin like a gentle rain.
It wasn't until her fourth climax he came again, falling to
her chest with a hoarse groan.

After several minutes, Thierry became vaguely
aware of Angelique stroking his hair. He had to be crushing
her, but every bone in his body felt as if it had melted.

"Am I hurting you?" he asked, nestling against her
breast. Damn, she felt good!

"Nope." She had never felt better. Any previous
doubts she might have had about his feelings were gone.
His feelings about her were evident in every touch, every
kiss.

"Angel, come away with me," he said after a few
minutes more. "Just for a week or so."

"Okay."

He was surprised. He'd thought she would have
questions, though he had no intention of telling her where
they were going. He had purposely left a made up receipt in

his desk at the office. Didier had told him about Lady Rienne contacting Linda after she was unable to get a hold of Piers, Aubrey, or Rance. She hadn't even attempted to get in touch with Remy.

"Can I ask you something?"

It wasn't like Thierry to sound unsure. Angelique went on instant alert.

"Yes," she responded cautiously.

"Where did you learn to do that? I mean, with your mouth . . . I mean . . . Shit." Well, he couldn't very well say, *Where did you learn to suck cock?,* now could he. He damn sure didn't want to imply she'd done it with anyone other than him. He knew she hadn't. "I am NOT implying anything, I just know you have never done it before."

"Was it that obvious?"

She sounded disappointed. Thierry rolled over, rolling her on top of him, forcing her to meet his eyes.

"No, it wasn't," he stated firmly. "I swear to you I have never had a—it has never been so sweet."

"Katrina taught me," she admitted, looking down.

"Katrina?"

Angelique nodded. "We used bananas."

"Bananas?" It was hard not to laugh out loud, but he was holding it together. He knew he shouldn't ask, but he had to. "What did you do with bananas after the uh, lesson?"

She looked up, confused. "We ate them."

CHAPTER FOURTEEN

"No one's seen Angelique?" Solange asked the three women assembled around table of the outdoor café.

"Nope," Katrina smirked, earning a little kick under the table from Regina.

"We all called," Jade supplied, unaware of the suspicions Angelique had shared Katrina and Regina before telling them she was going out of town with Thierry. They didn't know where, which was probably for the best. "Guess she's with Thierry."

Katrina snickered at the frustrated look on Solange's face, earning yet another kick. It was worth it in Katrina's mind. She had never liked Solange, or the way she was always telling her cousin what she should or should not be doing or who she should or should not be hanging out with. Katrina had been on to Solange years ago. She could spot a jealous bitch at fifty paces.

"I have to go," Solange told them, gathering her purse and keys.

"You just got here!" Jade exclaimed.

"There's something I have to do," Solange muttered, stomping off.

"Don't let us stop you," Katrina called after her pleasantly.

"Stop it!" Regina hissed at Katrina.

"You know the bitch only showed up today looking for information," Katrina defended. Angelique and Thierry had been gone for two days, and Solange had called three to four times a day, looking for her. Though Angelique hadn't gone into details, Katrina could feel there was definitely something going on. She was just glad her friend had finally thrown off the shackles her family had placed on her. It was about damn time the girl showed some fortitude against those calculating, prudish women.

"What the hell are you two talking about?" Jade demanded. She was definitely out of the loop here.

Regina rolled her eyes and filled Jade in. Angelique had told them they could share the information with Jade, just to make sure Solange wasn't around when they did it.

"So, where is she?" Jade asked after Regina finished telling her the story as she knew it.

"We don't know," Katrina told her before Regina had a chance to answer. "And it's best that we don't. I've never trusted that heifer for a second."

And Solange didn't trust any of the women she had left at the café table. She pulled out her cell as soon as she was out of sight to report in to her mother and aunt. Where the hell could Angelique be? They had to find her soon. Uncle Adam was furious with Aunt Charline for the way she had been treating his "precious child," and for telling Angelique the dirty little secret about her birth. It was a small miracle he had yet to fire Paul, but they all knew it was coming. It galled Solange to the bone that Angelique was handed everything on a silver platter, while she and her mother had to work and scheme for everything they had.

If only her father had lived longer, or had not been a debauched alcoholic asshole who single-handedly tried to populate the city with his little bastards, she might have had the advantages her cousin had. It just wasn't fair. Their grandmother had died, leaving Angelique a wealthy woman in her own right. The old woman hadn't trusted Charline for a second. Of course, she had known Charline had slept with Adam, Sr. long before she became the chosen bride for Adam, Jr. The old man had pushed his young mistress off on his son when Charline had declared she was pregnant. Unfortunately, she lost the child, and the ability to bear other children with it. To be fair, Solange's father was still alive when her grandmother had passed. She probably thought her son would take care of his wife and child instead of squandering his entire inheritance. When he died he had little more than family company stock, and most of that the bastard had split between her mother and his six illegitimate children. They barely had enough to keep them in their home.

And if Angelique didn't marry Paul, she and her mother were up shit creek.

*****

Arienne Chevalier hung up the phone slowly. Taking a several deep breaths, she leaned back against her chair. Her eyes cast blindly about the room she had made her own after the "death" of her husband. She didn't see the exquisite Victorian-era antique furniture, the tasteful blended hues of peaches, pinks, and soft grays. The family portraits that hung from the walls seemed to mock her, so she pointedly ignored their presence. Her grandsons perhaps had a right to be bitter. She had single-handedly removed all of their mothers from their lives at a very young age, preferring to raise them herself. She had done what was best for them. Why couldn't they see that? If she

hadn't, they would no doubt have fallen into the trap that

ensnared their grandfather, and that she could never allow.

All the women her sons had married were much too weak

to raise sons who bore the name Chevalier. She knew when

she married Albert she would do any and everything to

bring honor on the exalted name. Little did she know it was

Albert who would threaten it from within. And now, it was

Thierry.

What the hell was the point of having powerful sons

if they couldn't be depended on? First, Boden informed her

he was retiring from the military to come home and run

LeBlanc, Inc. She supposed she should be relieved Thierry

had decided to step down rather than drag the company

down with him. The boy simply didn't understand that

while the general public probably couldn't care who he

dated, their business partners, political contributors, and the

movers and shakers in their social circle would care a great deal. That Boden supported this nonsense was unconscionable! All of her sons had been old enough to understand what their father had done; they were there when he almost ruined this family! When she'd reminded Boden of that, he had dared to tell her it was hardly the same thing.

"Thierry is not married with children," he had sighed before rushing off the phone.

When she had called Beaumont to inform him of his son's perfidy, he had stated his son was old enough to make his own decisions about his life. Arienne had a sneaking suspicion Beaumont had talked to his son before she had a chance to. The good Senator had not been at all surprised by Arienne's news. It seemed her only two surviving sons had abandoned her. Rising heavily to her feet, Arienne poured herself a stout brandy. Maybe it was genetic, this damnable attraction to totally unacceptable women. *Women of color,* Arienne sneered to herself. There was something in the water here in Louisiana that made the forbidden so irresistible. Arienne was a Chevalier by birth herself; Albert had been a third cousin. She'd watched her own father fall victim to the same disease. Her mother had ignored her husband's infidelity as every lady worth her salt would. Arienne had done the same until the night Albert had told her he was leaving.

Shutting her eyes, Arienne shut out the memories best left in the past. Albert was long gone. He couldn't threaten her place in society anymore. Because of her age, she would perhaps be forgiven her grandson's foray into the forbidden. She just had to make damn sure this didn't become permanent. She had people looking for Thierry and his little tart in Paris. They would find him and bring him home by any means necessary. Until then, she had to think of a way to keep him away from Angelique Dubois for good. She was confident something would present itself.

After all, Lady Rienne was the master of manipulating her world and all who lived in it.

*****

Paul Guidry didn't like women. He never had. He liked fucking them, he used them, he manipulated them, but deep down he despised everything about them. They were feeble, foolish creatures. Hadn't his mother proven it when she'd fallen for a con man who wiped them out? She'd gleefully given her second husband complete control of the small fortune she'd inherited. By the time Paul had found out what she had done, it was gone, as was her husband. Maybe he could have used his advanced degrees to make enough to support his dim-witted mother and himself, but blackmailing Charline had been so much easier. The woman had all too readily handed over the keys to the Dubois kingdom, the mayor's daughter Angelique. It had been so easy to learn all of Charline's secrets. A little wine, a little seduction, and she was crying all over his shoulder.

293

But now Angelique was missing, and he was about lose his job. He had managed to avoid Adam so far, but his luck couldn't hold out for long. Rumors of Angelique and Thierry Chevalier were swirling around the city. Though no one had been so bold as to ask, he could feel curious eyes and looks of pity everywhere he went. Charline was no help, claiming her "daughter" was not answering her phone calls. There was something Charline wasn't telling him, but what?

Running out of options, Paul did the only thing he could at the moment. He called Solange.

Solange Dubois was the bane of his existence. Smarter than the average tart, she was blackmailing him while he was blackmailing her aunt. He had dated Solange before he left for college. Back then she had been a sweet little simpleton, or so he'd thought. She had found about his desperate need for funds and did a little investigating. She knew he was embezzling money. She knew he wanted to marry Angelique to gain controlling interests and hide his

theft. She probably knew he was paying Charline for her

daughter. If she wanted to keep the money she was

extorting from him coming, she had better help him.

*****

It took Thierry a minute to realize the pounding he

heard was coming from the front door of the hotel suite.

Checking to make sure Angel was still sleeping soundly, he

eased out of the bed and shrugged on his robe. There were

only two people who knew where he was, Remy and

Didier. So who the hell was at the door?   It was a relief

to see Remy, followed by Didier.

"You two do know it's four o'clock in the morning,

right?" Thierry groused, leading the two other men into the

suite's living room.

He had chosen to bring Angel to the Four Seasons

in Las Vegas rather than take her to the penthouse he

actually owned. The thought of taking Angel anywhere he had been with other women was distasteful.

"Your secretary ran to your grandmother with those fake receipts as planned," Didier told him, making himself comfortable in the only armchair in the room.

"And she dispatched a small army of knuckleheads to look for you," Remy added, stretching out on the couch. Thierry chose to remain standing.

"You came here to tell me that?" he asked irritably.

"Nope. We came to warn you the good Lady Rienne plans to have you committed when you get back to town," Didier told him, as if he'd just told him tomorrow would be hot in the desert.

"What?" Thierry would have been impressed by her ingeniousness of he weren't so damn pissed. "That sounds like something out of bad melodrama! How the hell does she think she could manage that?"

"Paid off a psychiatrist, stationed guards at every airport in Louisiana, and put the word out you were off your rocker," Remy told him. "Pissed off your daddy somethin' fierce. He's on his way up with Uncle Boden, by the way. They stopped at the front desk to check in."

Thierry dropped on the couch, shoving Remy's feet over as he did so. He expected a lot coming from Lady Rienne, but not this. It sounded so far-fetched that no one would believe it, which is exactly what she was counting on. There would be no way she could get to Angel and no way she could get to him. It was going to take some doing to outmaneuver the old lady this time.

Didier got up to let his father and uncle into the suite while Thierry sat deep in thought.

"So, where is the woman that has you so tied up you'd willingly bring down the wrath of your grandmother?"

Thierry looked up at the man who was his father. Truth be told, he hardly knew the man. That was by design of Lady Rienne, of course. She wanted her grandsons dependent on no one but herself. Unfortunately, she failed to realize that would only inspire them to depend heavily on themselves and each other. Maybe if she were capable of affection, things would have been different. However, Lady Rienne considered public displays of affection uncouth.

"Asleep like a normal person," Thierry muttered. He was glad he had decided to let his father and uncle know his plans. Whatever he decided to do about this latest news, it would definitely be easier with the elder Chevaliers on his side. Turning to Didier, he got back to the matter at hand. "What did you find out about Paul?"

"He's funneling funds from Dubois Enterprises into various offshore accounts," Didier answered. "He's also paying Charline, Solange and Anne Dubois several

thousand dollars a month from the money he's pilfering.
Adam is looking to fire him face to face, though he has no
idea the man has been stealing from him. Paul has managed
to avoid him for now. He and Charline hired a couple of
low-life types to find Angelique and bring her back. I have
no idea how they think they can force her to marry Paul
now, but they haven't given up."

"So, what are you going to do?" Uncle Boden
asked.

Hell if he knew. It was a little much to take in.

"I'm going back to bed," Thierry announced. "I'll
deal with the rest tomorrow. Feel free to stay as long as you
like."

He left all four men in the living room and returned
to the bed and the soft woman waiting there. Whatever he
decided to do, there was no way he was giving her up. He
had almost made it back to the bedroom when it hit him.
Marriage. He could protect Angel by giving her his name

while outmaneuvering Lady Rienne at the same time; all while gaining the one thing that would make him complete. From the first time he'd held her he knew she was home. All he could ever want or need in a petite, sexy little package. He had always planned on marrying her anyway. He hated to have to do it this way, but he would make sure she had the huge, extravagant ceremony all women seem to be so enamored of. The one thing he could do was make sure she at least had her friends here to stand by her. Tracing his steps back to the living room, Thierry set his plan in motion.

CHAPTER FIFTEEN

Thierry lay awake, waiting for Angel to wake up. He could hear people moving around and talking in what he supposed they thought was hushed tones outside the bedroom door. The suite had a living room, dining room, full kitchen and bar, media room and a walk-in closet, plenty of room for them to gather on the far side away from the bedroom door. Sighing, he gave himself a mental shake. He was anxious and just projecting his anxiety onto the people who had come to share what he hoped to be the best day of his life—if he could just do it without fucking up. Thierry wasn't used to asking for anything. He generally took what he wanted. But in this case, his future happiness lay entirely in the dainty hands of his Angel.

Angelique woke up slowly, stretching against the hard body beside her. The last several days had been pure magic. Thierry had taken her all over Las Vegas; shows on the Strip, dancing the night away at the best nightclubs,

even a hike in the desert. Here there were no sliding looks
or muttered comments. No one could have cared less who
she or Thierry were. Unfortunately, it had to end soon. As
much as she enjoyed being here with Thierry, New Orleans
was her home, and she'd be damned if she let anyone run
her out of it.

She was under no misconception that Charline had
given up on the idea of her marrying Paul. He had probably
found out that she wasn't Charline's child and was
blackmailing the older woman. What Angelique couldn't
figure out was why Paul wanted to marry her so badly.
There were other heiresses if money was what he was after.
Maybe it was Dubois Enterprises itself. She did own
controlling interests, and would one day inherit her father's
stocks as well. If that was what Paul wanted, that was just
too bad. She didn't give a damn whom he told about her
parentage, she wasn't going to be tied to a man she didn't
love, much less a snake of a man like Paul.

"What are you thinking about?" Thierry asked, pulling her closer and nuzzling her neck.

"What makes you think I'm thinking about anything?" she challenged back.

"You're biting your lower lip."

"I thought you said I did that when I'm horny." She laughed. It was funny how he knew her so well after such a short time. She was sometimes startled at how well they read each other's needs, how right they felt together.

"That's your top lip."

They lay for a few minutes more, just holding each other. Then Angelique became aware of delicious aromas coming from the other room, as well as people talking softly and moving around.

"Thierry, did you order breakfast? I though we were going out to eat this morning."

"That would be Remy, my father, and my Uncle Boden."

Among others, he mentally added. He didn't want to tell her about any of that yet, so instead he filled her in on all Didier had found out about her family, as well as his own. He was pleasantly surprised she wasn't at all shocked to find out Charline, her cousin, or her aunt. Smart woman, she had suspected the same thing. She was visibly upset over his grandmother's plans, muttering about telling the old woman a thing or two. By now, Uncle Boden had the doctor Lady Rienne had hired tied up in questioning by the F.B.I., deciding it was best to leave the guards she had stationed at the airports and fly into Mississippi. Then they would all drive into New Orleans to the most public restaurant to celebrate—that is, if things went as planned.

Thierry sighed. The idea had come to him as soon as he walked away from the other men. He went back to make arrangements, but he hadn't figured out how to get Angel to agree. He had practiced this over and over in his head before falling back to sleep early this morning. He couldn't mess this up.

"Marry me, Angel," he blurted before he lost his nerve.

Angelique stared with the wide-eyed innocence he had come to love. She had no idea how adorable she looked when she did that.

Kissing her little nose, he decided to cajole a little.

"I love you, Angel, baby. I don't want anyone but you, ever. I don't want you thinking I want to do this because of anything that is going on with my family or mine. I will not allow anyone to come between us, no matter what you decide. I want you with me every day and every night. I want you sleeping by my side. I want to spend my life making you happy, baby, I swear."

Angelique didn't know what to say. As much as she would like to say yes, she was scared. Scared he was asking her simply to protect her, or to get one over on his grandmother. She didn't doubt that Thierry loved her, for now. But what about tomorrow? She didn't want him to ever regret this decision.

"Thierry, I wouldn't want to move in the circles you move in," she warned. "And I have every intention of starting some kind of career as soon as we get back home."

"I don't give a damn what the world thinks, and I am not planning on moving in any circles but yours," he informed her. "Honey, I'm resigning. I have never liked my job or enjoyed what I do. I just never had anything else to do with my time."

"And what are you going to do now?"

Angelique shifted away from him and turned to watch him carefully. She would not go back to being an idle socialite, living for the next party or benefit. She wanted to do something substantial with her life. If Thierry didn't believe that or had discounted it, she didn't think she could continue seeing him, much less marry him, no matter how much she loved him.

"Since you're planning on going to work, I will just have to take care of you," he told her, gathering back in his arms. "Maybe I'll get Remy to teach me to cook. We might starve otherwise."

"And you'll paint, right? I think I'd like to be married to a temperamental artist." Her voice was muffled against his chest, but he heard her loud and clear.

She said yes! Thierry was so happy, he didn't even try to stop the tears that spilled down his cheeks. He had hoped and prayed, but until that moment, he'd been so scared she would say no. With all the things surrounding their relationship, he wouldn't have blamed her if she'd wanted to walk away from him and his certifiably insane family. He held on to her tightly, afraid to let go, afraid it was all a dream.

"God, I love you so much," he murmured. "I swear I will spend the rest of my life proving it to you."

*****

How strange, Angelique thought as she walked down the aisle, holding on to Thierry's father's arm. She had always thought to get married surrounded by her family, walking down the aisle with her own father. Yet here she was, surrounded by Thierry's cousins and her best friends; not exactly the family she had envisioned, but just right nonetheless. She was ecstatic Thierry had sent for Jade, Regina, and Katrina the night before. They were fast becoming the only family she could depend on. The three had been happy and encouraging about the wedding this evening. They had spent the day shopping for her gown, then their matching gowns, shoes, accessories, and Thierry's wedding ring. After the shopping trip, they had all met for a late lunch before preparing for the wedding.

Angelique was surprised at the complete acceptance by Thierry's father and uncle, given the lengths their mother was willing to go through to keep them apart. Beaumont and Boden were every bit as charming as the younger Chevaliers. Beaumont reminded her of J.R. from *Dallas*. He had salt and pepper hair, wicked blue-green eyes that remindered her so much of Thierry, and an inescapable aura of authority and power. He also had a wicked sense of humor that made you forget he was a United States Senator. Boden was a much younger version of his older brother, with serious deep blue eyes that seemed to miss nothing. He was every inch the general, quietly issuing orders that even his older brother obeyed without a conscious thought. Neither man was bothered in the least by Thierry's choice of wife.

Then there was the mysterious Didier. He didn't say much; he seemed to hang in the background, watching with an odd look of accomplishment. Thierry had just said he was a friend who found out valuable information for him; information like the fact that Paul was stealing from her father and blackmailing Charline. Other than that, all she could find out about him was that he used to work for Boden. Whether or not it was in the military was never made clear.

She had been a little apprehensive when Thierry had told her Remy would take care of all of the arrangements for the actual wedding. Just because this was Vegas didn't mean she would abide a cheesy wedding. No Elvis impersonators or crap like that. However, for the right price, even the Four Seasons had a chapel, complete with chaplain available for their guests.

The chapel was beautiful. Somehow the guys had managed to have it decorated with white and pink orchids and red roses and lit by white candles. She had chosen an ivory off the shoulder bustier-style silk gown, embroidered with tiny pearls and with a moderately long train. She had forgone a veil and left her hair down in a riot of tight corkscrew curls—at Thierry's request. Her three maids of honor wore simple black silk sleeveless sheath dresses that stopped right above the knee. Thierry stood waiting for her, his cousins by his side. She had no idea how he knew to wear a black cummerbund and tie. Probably because it would have matched anything. It was perfect. Her eyes watered at the thoughtfulness of her groom. She couldn't have loved him more than she did at that minute.

It was magic. Angelique couldn't look away from Thierry's shining eyes throughout the ceremony. She didn't remember repeating her vows, and she couldn't understand his at all. All she was aware of was Thierry; this magnetic man who had captured her heart and soul. Had it been a little over a month ago she was pining for someone to look at her like he was looking at her now?

All too soon, it was over. After the vows were said and a couple toasts were made, Angelique found herself swept into Thierry's arms as he made his way purposely to their suite.

"Hey," Angelique pouted as they entered the elevator, "I didn't even get any cake."

"Shit, I forgot the cake."

She had to laugh at the look of chagrin on his face. Just as he reached to return to the small banquet room where the others were celebrating, she grabbed his hand.

"No! I don't want to go back." Thierry let out a pent-up breath at her declaration.

God knows he didn't know how long he could last if he had to go back down and make merry. He wanted to be alone with his wife. Looking down at the woman in his arms, he felt his heart swell to bursting. His wife. Lord knew he had never done anything to deserve this precious gift heaven had given him. It humbled him that she had agreed to be his wife. He couldn't imagine what he'd have done if she'd said no, or worse, left him.

Angelique reached up and cupped his cheek. "I love you, Thierry," she whispered softly, offering her lips.

Thierry couldn't resist the invitation. Bending forward, he rubbed his lips over hers before placing a soft kiss on her mouth. He could not allow himself much more, not yet. It took a monumental amount of will, but he made it to the bedroom, the woman of his dreams in his arms. His hands shook as he moved to unlace the back of the gown. His wife; he was undressing his wife. Angelique watched him with ultimate trust and love in her eyes. How many times had he said to himself he didn't deserve that look? He had done nothing to deserve her love, to deserve a woman like her. She was sweetness and light; she embodied all that was good within him.

With patience he didn't really feel, he was able to peel off the gown carefully. When he gave her the wedding she deserved, she might want to wear it again. His heart stooped at the ensemble she had on underneath the silk confection. White satin and lace gleamed against the dark bronze of her skin, showcasing the intimate bustier that pushed her plentiful globes up, with matching panties that were not much more than a lace band holding a small triangle together.

"Oh, baby, you look good enough to eat," Thierry moaned, stopping to kiss the cleavage that seemed to taunt him.

Angelique laughed at the raw lust in her new husband's gaze. "That was the idea," she told him while undoing his tie, then unbuttoning his shirt.

It took little more than a flick of her wrist and a slight tug to remove the shirt and bare well-developed pecks, lightly sprinkled with the barest trace of dark hair. His dark burgundy nipples were every bit as excited to see her as she was them. Leaning forward to inhale his wonderfully masculine sandalwood scent, she flicked them lightly with her tongue, taking delight in the moan that escaped his lip. Angelique smiled as she felt a firm grip on the back of her head. Moving slowly to the other nipple, she felt the grip tighten as Thierry's breath caught. She bit down lightly, stepping closer to rub her body against the ever-growing erection in his pants. Dipping down, he gathered her closer, rubbing his cloth-clad pelvis against hers. He groaned again as he felt how wet she already was through her little panties and his trousers.

"Oh, Angel, baby, you're so wet for me," he whispered against her ear, smiling at her answering whimper. God, he loved to see her desperate, needy for a release only he could give. "Be a good girl and I'll make it all better."

Angelique sank to her knees in response, taking his pants with her. Before he could bring her back up, her lips wrapped around his throbbing cock and sank down, taking him all the way in, knocking the breath from his body.

"Oh, God!" Thierry groaned. He hadn't meant *that* kind of good girl!

She smirked to herself. She loved the powerful feeling of bringing him to his knees. She luxuriated in the way he first pulled at her hair, the way his body drew taut as she ran her tongue around the head of his cock, only to swallow him again the next second. She hummed deep in her throat, loving his responding groans.

"Stop, baby, I'm not going to last."

Pulling his penis from her mouth was the hardest thing he had ever had to do. It shivered at the sudden cold and jumped a little as if trying to find its way back into the warm, wet cavern of her mouth. Thierry picked her up and placed her in the middle of the bed, stripping her bare as he went. Remy, bless his twisted soul, had placed blood-red rose petals on the pure white cotton sheets he had requested from the concierge. God, she was breathtaking. He loved her full, high breasts with their pouty chocolate nipples, the way she dipped in at the waist only to curve out at her hips.

Climbing on the bed, he began to kiss her smooth skin from her neck, to her collarbone, to the valley between her breasts, down to her stomach. Angelique whimpered at the butterfly-soft touches to her skin, each one leaving a burning trail that led straight between her thighs. He didn't touch her throbbing nipples, but kissed his way around them, leaving her desperate. She tried to bow her back to get closer, frantic to feel his hot skin against her own, but he only moved away.

"Patience, sugar," Thierry chuckled at her frenzied attempt to bring him closer. He loved to see her like this, desperate in her need for him. He felt every bit as anxious, but he was determined to make his wedding night last. If he got too close now, he wouldn't be able to hold on to the tenuous control he had. Making his way to her thighs, he inhaled her scent. Fresh as the spring, yet intoxicatingly spicy. Nibbling on her inner thigh, he forced her legs open, smiling as they quickly wrapped around his shoulders. One long swipe from his tongue was enough to set her off.

"Oh, yeah, sugar. Show me how much you need me," he murmured, diving in, pressing his tongue deep inside her pussy.

He could feel her walls contracting in reaction to his small invasion. He moved his tongue up to swirl over her protruding clit while inserting two fingers deep inside her. Angelique couldn't hold back. The ruthless plundering of his fingers while he sucked on her clit like a starving man sent her crashing over the cliff. Smiling, Thierry kissed his way up her body to meet her own questing lips. Their mouths clashed with unsuppressed hunger. She tasted the sweet champagne mixed with her own juices on his tongue. Her hands clawed at his back, trying frantically to pull him even closer. His cock was poised right at her entrance, but he didn't descend.

"Please, Thierry, I need you so much!" Angelique heard herself beg.

He pushed in just enough to spread her open, and then stopped to suck on her nipples. She was mindless in her need, pushing her pelvis upward to seat him just a little more. It wasn't enough!

Thierry chuckled at her actions. "Bad girl. I told you you had to be a good girl; now you're going to have wait a little more."

With that, he withdrew completely. Moving down slightly, he cupped her breasts and concentrated on alternating between the two engorged nipples, suckling, licking, and biting lazily as if he had all the time in the world. His weight was settled on her lower body so she couldn't move. She felt like screaming in frustration when all of a sudden she felt the tension build again, climaxing once more.

"Now, that's a good girl. I think I'll reward you now."

Truth was, Thierry couldn't take it anymore. He had to bury himself deep inside her, or he might go insane!

Angelique cooed as he entered her slowly, stretching her inner muscles wide until every wonderful inch of his very generously-endowed cock was stuffed inside her. Her legs moved up so that her feet cupped against his ass, assisting his down strokes. Closing her eyes, she gave herself up completely to the milliard of feelings his lovemaking invoked. Her entire body was in flames, and he was only stoking the fire. She knew she was babbling nonsensical words, but she couldn't help it!

"Open your eyes, Angel, baby. Look at me."

Her eyes flew open at his command. Light and dark eyes clashed and held as they reached the zenith together, fusing their souls as well as their bodies.

"Mine," Thierry growled as he came harder than he ever had in his life. He'd thought the first time was spectacular, but nothing could ever compare to this! "My Angel."

CHAPTER SIXTEEN

Didier slid into the diner booth where Remy and Piers waited. They had chosen to meet far from the Strip, just in case. While Thierry and Angelique had been ensconced in their suite for the last forty-eight hours, the rest of them were busy at work, planning the couple's big entrance into New Orleans society as a couple. Rance had flown back right after the wedding to handle things on that end with the help of Angelique's three girlfriends. Aubrey was at the hotel with Boden and Beaumont. Both men thought it best if they returned with the happy couple, just in case Lady Rienne had found out her psychiatrist was no longer available to sign the commitment papers she had drawn up. Didier had gotten a disturbing report from the eyes he had on Paul and Charline. It shouldn't be a major problem, but it was something that couldn't be overlooked.

"Paul had a trace put on Angelique's credit cards. Apparently she used them to buy her wedding finery,"

Didier told the two assembled men. "And no one has seen
Solange for at least twenty-four hours."

"Do you think they would send her to bring
Angelique back?" Piers asked. It seemed unlikely.
Angelique had avoided her cousin like the plague before
leaving New Orleans. Surely they would have gotten a
clue.

"They don't know how much Angelique knows,"
Remy supplied, running it through his mind. "Still, I doubt
it. Solange has probably figured out the game is over and
lost. My guess is she skipped town."

"Possibly," Didier agreed. "We just need to make
sure someone is with Angelique at all times. They have
some serious criminal types looking for her. This doesn't
need to get messier than necessary."

"But she's married now." Piers didn't see the point
of Paul still trying to get to her. He couldn't force her to get
an annulment or divorce without Thierry's consent.

"They don't know that," Didier answered. "All we need to do is make sure they lay low until the public reception the night of their return. They will go straight there, then the good Senator will announce his son's marriage."

Although it seemed simple enough, Didier knew anything could go wrong. They all needed to handle this just right to avoid a hint of scandal. On Thierry's side of the family, all but Lady Rienne would be there. Now Rance had to make sure Angelique's mother and father would be there as well. He had managed to get Adam Dubois to meet the plane tomorrow evening at the airport in Mississippi. Angelique had insisted on being the one to break down the situation to her father. Didier agreed. The man had made some serious errors in judgment when it came to his daughter; she had every right to set him straight.

The men went over some last-minute details before heading in opposite directions. Remy and Piers went back to the hotel to wait until they flew out the next day. Didier

would be going back to New Orleans tonight. He had one

more mission to accomplish to make sure no one threatened

the newlyweds again.

*****

Solange grimaced at the tight hold on her arms.

"We're in an elevator; you can let go of my arm.

It's not like I can run anywhere."

The men holding her ignored her, as usual. How the

hell had she gotten herself into this situation? *By being a*

greedy, conniving bitch, she answered herself. The last

twenty-four hours had given her a lot to think about. She

should never have tried to bribe that bastard Paul. She

should have taken her money problems directly to Uncle

Adam, her mother's pride be damned. The woman had

been so emotionally scarred by her father that she couldn't

bring herself to trust or rely on another man. Unfortunately

that meant living by their combined wit. Well, apparently

they hadn't been too damn witty. She should have seen
there was something seriously off about Paul. Marrying
Angelique had become an obsession, even after Uncle
Adam had finally caught up with him to give him three
months to find other employment. He still had no idea Paul
was a thief.

She was on her way to tell him everything when she
had run into Aunt Charline. That was one seriously
disturbed woman. She had actually handed Solange over to
Paul and his goons. Charline seemed to be driven now by
hate; her hatred of Angelique, and her even more burning
hatred of her husband. Solange swore that if she got out of
this with her skin intact, she would never, ever do anything
the least bit shady again. Hopefully one day Angelique
would forgive her. They used to be so close when they
were young, before Anne and Charline's constant
disparaging of the other woman led Solange to falsely
believe Angelique had the life that should have been

rightfully hers. It was all bullshit, Solange realized now. Both women were emotionally scarred. They had almost succeeded in turning her into a sad reflection of themselves.

"We're here," one of the oafs announced. "Knock on the door."

Solange knocked, praying her cousin and her lover were not there. Her heart sank when Thierry threw open the door, wearing only loose pajama bottoms. On any other occasion, Solange might have taken a moment to thoroughly inspect the fine specimen of manhood in front of her. Right now all she could do was pray. *Oh, God, please let us make it out of this alive.* One of the oafs produced a gun and aimed it directly at Thierry's head.

"Thierry, who is it?"

Angelique came from the back just as the other intruder shut and locked the door. She had a towel wrapped around her otherwise naked body, her hair dripping in wet curls all around her face.

"Solange, what have you done?"

Solange couldn't meet the accusation in her cousin's eyes. Even if she hadn't orchestrated this, all this was partially her fault. She could have stopped it long ago.

"Take it easy," Thierry told the man closest to Angelique as he watched the man eyeing his wife with an interest that sent icy chills down his spine.

"Shut up!" the man holding the gun on him barked, pushing the nose of the gun against his forehead. "We are just gonna take yer girlfriend here back to her lovin' mama. If you shut the fuck up and do what we tell you, nobody's gonna get hurt."

Solange knew it was a lie. She was willing to bet everything she had that these men were former felons. They wouldn't leave any witnesses. She was just bait, and Thierry was a liability they didn't need. Too bad they weren't smart enough to realize his family was one of the most powerful in the country and would not rest until his murderers were themselves dead.

Watching the intruder next to Angelique carefully, Solange silently edged closer to the man next to Thierry. They only had one gun. If she could somehow disable the gun-wielding assailant, Thierry could take care of the man by the door—at least she hoped so. She'd heard Thierry was ruthless. She just prayed his mean streak wouldn't fail them all now.

"You're not taking her anywhere," came Thierry's rough, low voice. Solange shivered—and it wasn't even directed at her!

Oaf #1 looked surprised. He swallowed even as his grip tightened on the gun. Solange was close enough to see the sweat that began to bead on his brow. The way he was flexing his hands, she knew his palms were sweating too. Taking as deep a breath as she dared, she suddenly fell sideways, putting all her weight on the unsuspecting man.

Thierry moved with perfect timing, grabbing his wrist and bending backwards with such force Solange heard the slight pop. Thierry aimed the gun directly at the man who had dared to threaten his wife, his finger tightening on the trigger before the man had a chance to move. The deafening shot was obscenely loud, then absolute silence. Scurrying back from the fallen assailant, Solange could see he had passed out cold while the other man had breathed his last. For a full minute there was absolute stillness, before the door was burst open by security and a large man with flowing dark hair Solange had never seen before.

It was Thierry who moved first. Moving to his wife's side, he gathered her in his arms while he buried her face into his chest. The armed security guards began falling all over themselves, asking forgiveness for the serious breech of security while gathering up the fallen men. No one noticed Solange. She quietly made her way towards the open door, thinking of disappearing entirely She had almost made it out of the door when a giant, forceful hand landing

on her shoulder. She looked up, and up some more to see

an older version of Thierry looking down at her. He looked

far too young to be his father, but he was too old to be one

of the cousins.

"Goin' somewhere, sweetheart?"

Solange swallowed harshly and shook her head.

Damn it! She had almost made it. Now she was forced to

sit and watch as the security guards kissed ass in a major

way to the Chevaliers gathering in the room. The hotel

manager had made his way upstairs to assure the newly-

married couple of another suite—free of charge, of course.

Strange how no one seemed to ask any of the Chevaliers

what had happened. They just assumed the men had been

trying to rob affluent guests. The fact that Solange had been

with them had not been mentioned. Thank God for that, at

least. She had no doubt there would be hell to pay when the

hotel staff left.

Solange's eyes snapped toward her now-dressed cousin and the man at her side as they solemnly answered question and directed staff to the removal of their personal belongs from the suite. Married? Of all the things Solange had imagined Angelique might be doing with Thierry in Vegas, marriage had never been one of them. It should have been; people often ran to Vegas for a quickie marriage or a quickie divorce. It was something she'd never dreamed her cousin would do.

All too soon, Solange found herself escorted into another unbelievable suite even more posh than the last, where she faced not only her cousin and her new husband, but Senator Chevalier, General Boden Chevalier, and the same unidentified man with the flowing ebony hair. Hoping to head off the storm she suspected was coming, she began in a rush.

"I swear, I didn't lead them here. I know you are probably well aware of my involvement with Paul . . .

about the embezzling, I mean. But I swear I never wanted to see you seriously hurt, Angel."

"No, you just wanted to make sure I married a lying thief who would have made my life miserable." Angelique wasn't as mad as she thought she would be when she finally confronted her cousin. Instead, she felt a sad sense of loss. They had been very close before puberty. There had been a time when she felt Solange was her only friend. Too bad money and position were more important to the other woman. Sighing, Angelique decided she wanted to get this over with as soon as possible. She had no desire to punish Solange, however much she might have deserved it. She just wanted this whole business behind her. She wanted to get on with her life. She would never trust her cousin again, but she would not let this destroy them all. Hopefully, Solange would take this second chance to become a better person. Angelique doubted it, but she was willing to give her that chance.

Reading the weariness in Angelique's body language, Thierry decided to save the conversation for a later time. Angel had been through too much, and there was more to come tomorrow.

"Didier, how did you know to come back?" Thierry asked.

Didier shrugged. "I saw her at the airport. I had chartered a small plane to go back when I saw her and the two guys with her disembarking from a private plane. She didn't look too happy. My sources hadn't reported anyone looking for her, though I knew she hadn't been seen for a couple days. So, I followed them. I couldn't follow too closely, they would have made me. Unfortunately, I was too late."

"No," Angelique interjected. "You were right on time. There is no use going over it again and again. In the end, Solange did help, and Thierry saved the day. Let's just let it go at that."

Angelique turned to go, Thierry following her. Making eye contact with Didier, he nodded toward Solange, his message evident. *Don't let her out of your sight.* The couple left to their new room, leaving Solange with a group of strange men who could not be too happy with her right now.

"What are you going to do with me?" She managed to sound clear and unafraid, though nothing could be farther from the truth.

"Nothing." This came from Boden, the general. He was looking at her with some kind of fascination she didn't quite understand and was completely unnerved by. He wanted something, but what was anyone's guess.

"So, I can leave?" She hated how hopeful her voice sounded, but damn it, she was of no use to any of them. Sure, she could have run straight to her aunt or Paul to tell them of the latest developments, but she just wanted to be as far away from this situation as she could get! "I will not

335

go anywhere near New Orleans, I swear!" Hating the pleading tone she heard in her voice, she crossed her fingers and surveyed the room. It was not encouraging. There would be no escaping for her.

"On the contrary," Boden told her, "you will be returning to New Orleans. With us. Until this thing is completed, I don't think I will be letting you out of my sight."

Solange quaked at his statement. She had no idea what these people were planning, but she did know the tone of Boden Chevalier's voice held a promise, one that did not look like something she was going to enjoy.

CHAPTER SEVENTEEN

Angelique closed her eyes as she rested her head on Thierry's shoulder. Thank God this was almost over. She was going to need a very long vacation after tonight. Though the drive wasn't really that long between Mississippi and New Orleans, it had been a long day. Their entire entourage had stopped at a large property owned by Rance outside of Hidden Island, right near the Mississippi border. They had met Adam Dubois there, instead of at an airport as originally planned. Angelique had been left alone with her father, as per her request. She informed him of her wedding, of Paul's theft, and the attempted abduction, as well the night's festivities. She had explained exactly what she expected of him. He would be at the reception, as would his wife, smiling benignly in love and acceptance. They would present a united front. Afterwards, when she was ready to talk to him, she would let him know. She also made it very clear to keep his wife away from her and out of her life. As contrite as Adam was, Angelique was too tired of dealing with other people's issues.

Now they were all dressed to kill and on their way to the Royal Sonesta Grand Ballroom. Thierry's father and uncle were already there, as were Adam and his wife, Aunt Anne, Solange, Jade, Regina, Katrina, Aubrey, Piers, and Remy. Rance was riding up front of the stretch limo with the chauffeur. The party had been in full swing for about an hour now. It was important for Thierry and Angelique to make a grand entrance.

"I forgot to give you your wedding gift." Thierry broke the silence of the ride, handing Angelique a thin shirt size box.

Angelique took the box with slightly quivering hands. "You didn't have to," she began, unable to finish for fear of bawling her eyes out. In the short time they had been together, this man had shown her in so many ways how a man treats the woman he loves. She opened the

package to stare at the sheaf of papers. Thierry turned on
the overhead light so that she could read them.

"The Angel Foundation? Thierry, what is this?"

As she read further, she couldn't stop a tear or two
from escaping. "You set this up for me?"

"Well, you made it clear you were tired of being
nothing more than some kind of spokesmodel for charities.
Every time you started talking about going into business,
the conversation always wound up being about some sort of
cause rather than a money-making endeavor. We don't
need any more money, so I thought maybe you'd like to run
your own foundation."

He was right. As much as she wanted to do
something with her life, she was far more interested in
helping others than she was with making more money for
the sake of making money.

"Oh my God, is that my beginning budget!?"
Angelique started at the seven-figure sum in awe.

"We will, of course, hit up as many people as we can tonight." Thierry smiled. "Set it up as an alternative to wedding gifts."

Angelique threw herself into his arms. "Thank you! Thank you so much! This means more to me than . . . "

Thierry knew exactly how she felt. Setting up the foundation instead of creating some kind of business had been a wise idea. Angelique was a generous, passionate woman. Giving her the opportunity to do good in a way she chose would make her happy and help her use skills she had never been able to utilize before. Her goodness really humbled him. Being married to an actual Angel was going to be an education in itself, and a hell of a lot of fun.

*****

Didier sat behind the desk in the darkened room, listening the sounds of his quarry coming closer. She was understandably upset. By now she knew of her sons' little

soirée. She was an intelligent woman; she would guess
what it meant.

"I don't care where Dr. Tibbett is! I want him here
now!"

The door opened, lights blazed, and Lady Rienne
stopped dead when she saw who was sitting behind her
desk.

"What the hell are you doing here?" she demanded,
not moving any closer to the desk.

"Oh, you already know, Arienne." Didier smiled. It
was petty to taunt her, but her intense dislike of his
presence, coupled with the fact there wasn't a damn thing
she could do about it, gave him a little rush. He had tried to
like the woman. He had tried to work with her, but her
hatred of everything he was made that impossible. She
didn't blame her for hating his grandfather; she had earned
that right, in a way. But he had nothing to do with anything
that went on before his birth.

"He married that—"

"Careful," Didier warned, not allowing her to finish the inflammatory statement. "Yes, Thierry and Angelique are married. Their reception is tonight at the Royal Sonesta. You need to get changed so we can be on our way."

"I WILL NOT. . ."

Didier came to his feet and stalked toward the bitter old woman. To her credit, she didn't cringe or back down, though she knew she had lost. "You will. Beaumont and Boden will not hesitate to welcome their father back into the fold should *Grand-péré* decide to come and make a sudden appearance. You don't really want to drag all the family's dirty laundry out into the full light of day, do you?"

Arienne stiffened. Of course she could not have that. Not while she still drew breath. When she was dead and gone they could do what they wanted, but she would not be humiliated like that.

"I will go, but I will not speak and give verbal blessings to this travesty."

Arienne turned on her heel and stalked from the room. Didier had to admire her moxie. He wondered if she would be able to bounce back this quickly after the next one.

EPILOGUE

Thierry watched quietly as his wife went over financial statements of the growing charity organization she chaired. His chest swelled with pride as he thought of all she had conquered. Here she was, running a major organization, when just a short time ago she was a shy, almost retiring debutante. Now she bullied local, national, and even international businesses into funding the rebuilding of her beloved New Orleans, whereas before she wouldn't even stand up to her own mother. *Stepmother*, he silently corrected himself.

As much as he would have liked to take some credit for his Angel coming out of her shell, he knew that it was something she had done all on her own. She had made the decision to stand up for herself and to take charge of her own life. He just thanked God her choice included him. Thierry smiled ruefully. Angelique Dubois Chevalier was one hell of a woman, even standing up to his dragon of a grandmother, enlisting her help in aiding those misplaced by Hurricane Katrina; people his grandmother would have never have spit on had they been on fire.

"For family appearances," Angelique had told Lady Rienne, *"you will donate from your personal funds, as well as come to every opening, every gala, every fundraiser. No matter whom Thierry might have married, the Chevalier name still means a lot in Louisiana."*

"And if I don't?" Lady Rienne sniffed. *"What can you possibly do to me?"*

"Why, I wouldn't do a thing," Angelique replied sweetly. *"However, should the gossip columnists catch wind of all you tried to do to stop this wedding . . ."* she shrugged. *"You're the one who would have to deal with the fallout. Not Thierry, and definitely not me."*

Lady Rienne gave his wife wise berth now.

Putting away his sketchpad, Thierry moved from his seat by the window to the big leather easy chair beside the desk where Angelique was working.

"Come here, baby," Thierry said huskily.

Angelique looked up from her calculations and smiled at the look in her husband's eyes. Lord, that man could turn her on with just a glance. She only made it within the reach of his arms before Thierry reached out to pull her down across his lap, his lips taking hers with every bit as much passion as the first time.

"I love you, Mrs. Chevalier," Thierry murmured against her lips.

"And I love you, Mr. Chevalier," she responded. "You're my hero."

Thierry smiled down at the best thing that had ever happened to him. "You, sugar, are my very own Angel."

About The Author

Shara Azod is a proud graduate of Trinity University, where she acquired her B.S. in Business Administration. She also spent four years serving in the Navy. She has traveled extensively, but her favorite destination is Paris (of course!). Bahrain, Hong Kong, and Sicily are very close favorites.

She fell in love with romance novels at the age of 13 after reading The Flame and the Flower. Her first attempt at romance was three binders of an ongoing saga feature herself and the members of Duran Duran.

She is currently married with two gorgeous children. She met her husband in Japan, they shared their first date in Hawaii, and they later married in San Diego. She's lived in Southern California, Chicago and Sicily. She currently resides in the south.

Shara loves to hear from her fans, so feel free to email her anytime! To learn more about Shara Azod please visit her at www.sharaazod.com or www.cacoëthespublishing.com/sharaazod. Send an email to Shara at sharaazod@gmail.com.

Look for these titles by Shara Azod...

Coming Soon:

Remy Goes to Therapy

People perceive him as a playboy. Her friends see her as a prude. What will happen when you put these two together?

Remy Goes to Therapy

© 2008 Shara Azod
Coming 2008 from Cacoethes Publishing House, LLC.

"I know what you're afraid of." Remy's voice deepened with retrained desire. He used his natural southern drawl with devastating effects. His words tended to wash over the skin in a smooth caress. Regina squirmed uncomfortably, trying to concentrate on anything but the way he made her want to melt.

"I am afraid you have mistaken me for someone else." She was inordinately proud of the way she sounded: clear, concise, and in complete control. It wouldn't do at all to let him know he was getting to her.

"I know exactly who you are, Dr. Regina Belle Booker."

Regina cringed. How the hell had he managed to find out her middle name? More importantly, why would he want to? *You're playing with the big boys now, Regina Belle.*

"What exactly do you want from me, Mr. Chevalier?" She used her best doctor-to-patient voice. The one that projected authority. That generally worked to cool off the most amorous advances.

Remy frowned. He hadn't planned on backing her into the corner. He had only wanted to see her ruffled a little. He knew better than to try for anything more with Dr. Booker. She specialized in digging into a person's innermost thoughts. He had skeletons best left dead and buried. He didn't want to let it go, though. There was something about Regina that dared him. Just once, he needed to see her lose control a little. That, or take that damn bun down.

"I want you to admit you're afraid," he told her, shifting so his growing erection rubbed against her even more. She ignored it.

"Afraid of what, exactly?"

She sounded exasperated. Good. At least now she was showing some kind of reaction. Not the kind of emotions he was looking for, but for some reason he needed this woman to respond to him.

"You're afraid I might be too, uh, much for you to handle," he smirked.

If you only knew, Regina thought. "Excuse me?"

"You know, the white man/ big . . . attribute thing," Remy replied with a perfectly straight face. You don't have to worry, *chere*. I know it might be somewhat larger than the norm, but I swear, I'll be real careful."

Cacoethes Publishing House, LLC.
(cacoethes=uncontrollable desire)

Action/Adventure
Fantasy
Historical
Horror
Mainstream
Mystery/Suspense
Non-Fiction
Paranormal
Romance
Science Fiction
Western
And Much, Much More!

http://www.cacoëthespublishing.com